WEARING NOTHING BUT HIS HELMET, HIS SWORD, HIS WAISTCOAT AND A TEENY-WEENY PAIR OF HAIRY SWIMMING TRUNKS, HICCUP HORRENDOUS HADDOCK THE THIRD HAS BEEN KIDNAPPED!

But his outfit is the least of his worries. Trapped on *The American Dream II* with his friends Fishlegs and Camicazi, Hiccup must **ESCAPE** the barbarian Norbert the Nutjob, and somehow dodge the cruel **POLAR-SERPENTS** in the icy waters below.

If **ONLY** Hiccup hadn't promised to help the Wanderer slaves on board escape too! **HOW** will Hiccup save himself, his friends and a hundred and twenty-two Wanderers off a ship **WITHOUT** their terrifying captors noticing?

You don't **HAVE** to read the Hiccup books in order.
But if you want to, this is the right order:

1. How to train your Dragon
2. How to be a Pirate
3. How to speak Dragonese
4. How to Cheat a Dragon's Curse
5. How to Twist a Dragon's Tale
6. A Hero's Guide to Deadly Dragons
7. How to Ride a Dragon's Storm
8. How to Break a Dragon's Heart
9. How to Steal a Dragon's Sword
10. How to Seize a Dragon's Jewel
11. How to Betray a Dragon's Hero
12. How to Fight a Dragon's Fury

JOIN HICCUP ON HIS QUEST
(although he doesn't quite realise he is on one yet...)

THE PROPHECY OF
THE KING'S LOST THINGS

'The Dragontime is coming
And only a King can save you now.
The King shall be the
Champion of Champions.

You shall know the King
By the King's Lost Things.
A fang-free dragon, my second-best sword,
My Roman shield,
An arrow-from-the-land-that-does-not-exist,
The heart's stone, the key-that-opens-all-locks,
The ticking-thing, the Throne, the Crown.

And last and best of all the ten,
The Dragon Jewel shall save all men.'

Hiccup

Toothless

Stormfly

Snotlout

BIG BOOBIED BERTHA

MadGUTS the Murderous

Gumboil, Madguts' assisstant

NORBERT
the
Nutjob

Fishlegs
(Hiccup's
best
friend)

Camicazi

Stoick the
Last

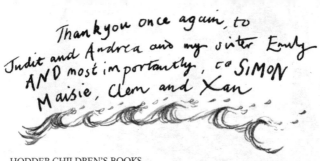

Thank you once again, to Judit and Andrea and my sister Emily AND most importantly, to SIMON Maisie, Clem and Xan

HODDER CHILDREN'S BOOKS

First published in Great Britain in 2008 by Hodder & Stoughton
This edition published in 2017 by Hodder & Stoughton

1 3 5 7 9 10 8 6 4 2

SPECIAL EDITION

Text and illustrations copyright © 2008 Cressida Cowell

A CIP catalogue record for this book is available from the British Library.

ISBN: 978-1-444-93982-8

Cover design by Jennifer Stephenson
Background cover illustration by Christopher Gibbs

Printed and bound by Clays Ltd, St Ives Plc

The paper and board used in this book are made from wood from
responsible sources.

MIX
From responsible
sources
FSC
www.fsc.org   FSC® C104740

Hodder Children's Books
An imprint of Hachette Children's Group, Part of Hodder & Stoughton
Carmelite House, 50 Victoria Embankment, London EC4Y 0DZ
An Hachette UK Company
www.hachette.co.uk

To Stephen, Joanna, Chloe, Nell and Michael, my American cousins, with love

Great West Ocean

How to Ride a
Dragon's Storm

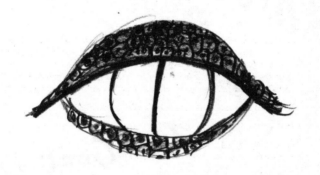

written and illustrated by
CRESSIDA COWELL

Hodder
Children's
Books

A division of Hachette Children's Group

THE LAND OF THE POLARSERPENTS

the Murderous Mountains ↓

the little isle of BETH

THE BARBARIC ARCHIPELAGO

~ CONTENTS ~

THE CURSE OF BEARCUB'S GRANDMOTHER

A long time ago, a small boy was dreaming.

He was dreaming of running through the beautiful white wilderness that was his childhood home, running and running through snow so perfect you could hardly bear to touch it. But suddenly his legs grew tired and so heavy he could hardly move them... something was pulling him back... what was it?

And then he awoke and opened his eyes, and he was about as far from home as he could possibly be, lying in the darkness below the decks of a great ship.

The boy was called Bearcub. He belonged to a people called the Northern Wanderers, and he had not always been a slave. Only two weeks before, he had had miles and miles of glorious icy desert to play in, as free as the polar bears and seals that his people harpooned to eat and keep them warm.

But then the Vikings came.

They had surprised the Wanderers by attacking while they were asleep, dragging them aboard their Viking ships and taking them away from their homeland. Since that time, Bearcub had not had a proper meal, and worse still for a boy full of fidgets and used to running, he hadn't taken more than a couple of steps.

Bearcub's father had been out on a hunting party when the Vikings struck so he had not been captured.

'Please father,' Bearcub whispered into the blackness. 'Save me, father...'

'HA!' rasped the doom-filled furious voice of Bearcub's scary Grandmother, who was lying chained beside him. 'Your father cannot rescue you, for he does not know where you are. And the gods must have forgotten us, to let this happen. Vikings are vermin, every single one of them,' she spat into the darkness. 'I never met a good one. Murderous, wicked, evil people... oh, if I had one here I would do such things. I could eat their livers I really could. I am Cursing this voyage and everyone aboard this ship...'

'WE are aboard this ship,' Bearcub pointed out. 'Do not Curse this voyage or you may be Dooming us, too.'

'YOU do not contradict your elders and betters,' cried his Grandmother sternly (it is not pleasant to be chained to a cursing Grandmother). 'We are DOOMED already... No, the only thing left for us now is to Hate, and to Curse...'

And so Bearcub's Grandmother had ALL of the
Wanderers Hating, and Cursing, and wanting to eat
people's livers, baying out their fury in the rocking
darkness below the decks of the ship.

'YOU BETTER WATCH YOUR STEP UP THERE!'
screamed Bearcub's Grandmother, howling up at the
ceiling like a wolf. 'IF ONE OF YOU MISSES YOUR
FOOTING AND FALLS DOWN THAT HATCH, I'M
TELLING YOU, WE'LL TEAR YOU APART!'

Only Bearcub was quiet, and in the blackness no
one could see the tears slowly rolling down his cheeks,
which was lucky, because Wanderers have the hearts of
polar bears and they do not cry.

And inside his head he repeated over and over
again, 'Please, father,
please, help me... please,
gods, please, please, help
me... please... anybody...
if you're listening...
help me... help me...
help me...'

help
me.

tick
tock
tick
tock

1. A PROPER VIKING SWIMMING RACE

One chilly spring day in the Barbaric Archipelago, Hiccup Horrendous Haddock the Third, the Hope and Heir to the Tribe of the Hairy Hooligans, was standing miserably on the West Beach of the Murderous Mountains with absolutely nothing on but his helmet, his sword, his waistcoat, and a teeny weeny pair of hairy swimming trunks.

The Murderous Mountains were not the kind of place you wanted to visit at the best of times. They gave Hiccup the shivers. Tall, cruel-looking, dizzyingly high peaks that were home to some unspeakably dangerous dragons and mutant wolves, not to mention the Murderous Tribe, the fiercest and most ruthless Vikings in the uncivilised world.

The Murderous Tribe did not often receive visitors. Perhaps it was their uncomfortable habit of sacrificing unwelcome intruders to the Sky Dragons at the point of Mount Murderous that kept people at bay.

But on this occasion, Madguts the Murderous had taken it into his head to be hospitable, and to invite two of the other Tribes, the Hooligans and the Bog-Burglars, over to his island for a jolly little

19

Inter-Tribal Friendly Swimming Race.

It was a traditional *Viking* Swimming Race, and the Vikings were a little bit crazy, so they were going swimming with their weapons on: swords, axes, daggers, that sort of thing.

It did not seem to have occurred to them that this would make them less floaty.

So there they were, the entire Warrior populations of the Murderous, Hooligan and Bog-Burglar Tribes, hopping up and down on the uncomfortable shingle beach, trying to pretend they

weren't freezing their horns off, with the mutant wolves howling cheeringly up in the mountains above.

There was a strong easterly wind that brought goose-bumps to Hiccup's skinny, freckled arms, and whisked off helmets, cloaks and swords, and sent them bowling briskly down the beach. Hiccup's tiny hunting-dragon, Toothless, was having difficulty flying without being blown away.

Toothless
was a particularly
small Common-
or-Garden dragon
with large,
innocent greengage eyes.

'Toothless w-w-wouldn't go swimming today if Toothless was you,' he advised Hiccup. 'Is very ch-ch-chilly in there, Toothless has been in already and it nearly froze Toothless's wings off.'

'Yes, thank you, Toothless,' said Hiccup. (Hiccup was one of the very few Vikings, before or since, who could speak Dragonese, the language in which the dragons speak to each other.) 'Very helpful, I'll bear that in mind.'

Gobber the Belch, the teacher in charge of the Pirate Training Programme on Berk, had stripped down to his smalls, and was breathing in the gale as if it were the loveliest of summer breezes. 'Lovely swimming weather!' he roared delightedly, beating his chest with his fist like a great red-headed gorilla. 'Gather

T-t-t-oothless want to go H-home... Is ch-chilly.

round and stand to attention, boys, and I'll explain the Rules of the Race…'

The twelve boys stood before their teacher in a shivering line.

Toothless was in a big grump

'Now boys!' boomed Gobber. 'A Proper Viking Swimming Race is not like those pathetic little competitions they carry out on the mainland. It is a test of your ENDURANCE, your STRENGTH and your SUICIDAL BRAVERY…'

'Oh brother,' moaned Hiccup's best friend Fishlegs, who was the only boy on the Programme who was even worse than Hiccup at all the Viking activities. He had legs as limp as two strings of spaghetti, and he couldn't swim. 'I don't like the sound of this…'

'In a proper Viking Swimming Race,' continued Gobber, 'the winner is the person who is LAST.'

There were gasps of surprise, and 'oh sir, please sir, that can't be right, sir,' from the line of boys.

'In which case,' sneered Snotface Snotlout, a great bullying brute of a boy whose muscly arms were covered entirely in skeleton tattoos, 'Hiccup the Useless will win, no problem. *He's* always the last at everything…'

Hiccup stood on one leg, tried to smile, and fell over in the sand.

'*Aha*,' grinned Gobber, his beard bristling with keenness. He laid one finger to his nose. 'But think carefully about this, boys... we all set out from the beach and start swimming, and from then on it's a game of Chicken. Who can swim out the furthest, the longest, into the deepest ocean, and still return? Many are the Warriors over the centuries who in their pride have misjudged the swim BACK, and who have drowned as a consequence...'

'Oh yippee...' moaned Fishlegs.

'But on the plus side, anyone who drowns in the course of a Swimming Race will automatically go straight to Valhalla,' smiled Gobber, in the manner of someone giving everybody a great big birthday present.

'Oooooooooooh,' exclaimed the boys in a pleased way.

'MAD,' groaned Fishlegs, swaying in the wind like a small skinny tree about to snap. 'We are the only sane people in a Tribe of total LOONIES.'

Fishlegs

'Any questions?' roared Gobber.

Hiccup put up his hand. 'A small point, sir. Won't we freeze to death in about five minutes?'

'Don't be a softy!' roared Gobber. 'The Blubberwing fat you have rubbed all over you SHOULD keep you warm enough to prevent actual DEATH... but it's all part of the game, of course. Can you use your skill and judgement to stay out long enough to win the Race... but not SO LONG that you freeze to death?'

Gobber walked up and down the line of boys inspecting them before they went out to join the competition. 'Very smart, Snotlout... Chin up, Tufnutt Junior... Haven't you forgotten something, Clueless?'

'I've got my sword, sir,' said Clueless.

'You do have your sword,' admitted Gobber, 'but you DO NOT have your swimming costume. Put it on quick, boy... I don't think that Thor will be welcoming you into Valhalla in the altogether. It really doesn't bear thinking about...'

He moved along the line until he stopped dead in front of Fishlegs. 'WHAT,' roared Gobber in an awful voice, 'WHAT in Thor's name are THESE?'

'Armbands, sir,' replied Fishlegs, looking straight ahead.

'Fishlegs can't swim, sir,' offered Hiccup in defence of his best friend. 'So we made him these out of a couple of pig bladders. Otherwise he sinks like a stone.'

'Like a stone,' repeated Fishlegs helpfully.

'Oh for Woden's sake,' blustered Gobber, 'what are the Murderous Tribe going to think if they catch sight of THOSE? I'll lend you my cloak, Fishlegs, and you can drape it over them, and let's just hope nobody notices. Thor give me strength...

Luckily, the Hooligan boys were very sensitive about these things...

HA! HA! HA! HA! HA!

'Now, has everybody got their hunting-dragon?' bellowed Gobber.

The boys had brought their hunting-dragons. They were huddled on the beach, their wings over their heads, shielding themselves from the rain.

'Your hunting-dragon can fly over your head as you swim. It makes you easier to spot from the beach, and they can maybe fight off any predators… sharks, Darkbreathers, that sort of thing… OK, you can fall out now and get ready, and I'll see you at the start line in about five minutes.'

The boys began their last-minute preparations, chattering excitedly.

'Hi there, LOSERS,' sneered Snotlout, a tall, mean boy with nostrils so large you could stick a cucumber up them (Toothless had actually DONE this once) and the repellent beginnings of a moustache sprouting on his upper lip like a little hairy caterpillar. 'I hope ickle baby Hiccup has been practising his doggy-paddle then…'

He gave Hiccup a big shove that sent him sprawling in the sand.

'Her her her…' snorted Dogsbreath the Duhbrain, Snotlout's equally unpleasant sidekick. Dogsbreath looked rather like a gorilla in goggles who had been over-doing it with the doughnuts.

'Very funny, Snotlout,' replied Hiccup, spitting sand out of his mouth.

'You guys are normally so good at coming in last...' sneered Snotlout. 'In fact this may be your only opportunity ever to come in FIRST, for once... Just try and at least go out of your depth, won't you, before you crawl back to the beach like the pathetic cowardly little plankton you are? You don't want to embarrass us PROPER Hooligans more than you actually have to... Nice armbands, Fishlegs, by the way...'

And Dogsbreath took the pot of slimy green Blubberwing goo Fishlegs was holding in his hands and poured it over Fishlegs's head, before strolling off with Snotlout, who had a rather basic sense of humour, and was laughing so hard he could barely walk.

'I hope a Darkbreather gets him,' said Fishlegs gloomily, taking off his glasses and trying to rub off the Blubberwing fat

with the edge of his swimmers, but only succeeding
in smearing it all over the glass so that they were
impossible to see through.

'It would just spit him out again,' replied Hiccup
even more gloomily, trying to rub the sand off himself,
but completely failing because the Blubberwing fat was
so sticky. 'I bet he tastes horrible.'

PAAAAA-AARAAAP!

A musician from the Murderous Tribe sounded
the horn to summon the competitors to gather for the
beginning of the Swimming Race...

The Blubberwing goo
had so attached itself to
the glass that it was like
looking through a dense pea-green
FOG

2. MAY THE FATTEST (AND LEAST STUPID) MAN (OR WOMAN) WIN

Hiccup's father and grandfather came over to the boys to wish them luck.

Hiccup's father, Stoick the Vast, O Hear His Name and Tremble, Ugh, Ugh, was the Chief of the Hairy Hooligan Tribe. He was built in the traditional Viking mould, six-and-a-half-feet high, belly like a battleship, eyebrows blowing in the breeze like a couple of large hamsters doing cartwheels. He was horribly hearty, and full of the joys of spring.

'Fabulous day for a Swimming Race!' he roared happily.

'I'm not sure I agree with you,' wheezed Old Wrinkly, Hiccup's grandfather, who was one of the Judges in the competition. He was a wrinkled old oyster of a man, whose ancient back had been blown into a hoop by ninety years of Archipelago gales. His long tangly white beard trailed behind him, picking up shells and seaweed as it dragged in the sand.

Old Wrinkly had been trying to persuade Stoick not to take part in the Race.

'I have been looking into the Future and the Omens are not good,' whispered the old man.

'NONSENSE!' pooh-poohed Stoick the Vast. 'Everyone knows you're hopeless at looking into the Future, Old Wrinkly. Now, *I'm* obviously going to win this Race,' said Stoick, who didn't do modesty, 'but, Hiccup, I would like YOU to beat Snotface Snotlout and that sort of thing...'

Snotface Snotlout was Hiccup's cousin. He was a good foot-and-a-half taller than Hiccup, incredibly muscly and tough, and better at Hiccup at practically everything. Hiccup had no chance of beating him in a Swimming Race.

But Stoick often didn't notice things like that.

Stoick gave Hiccup a kindly biff on the shoulder. 'I KNOW you can do it, son!' he said enthusiastically. 'You may be small, but you're wiry! And your legs might be just a trifle on the skinny side, but you've got the old Horrendous Haddock *fight* in those knobbly knees! All you have to remember, lad,' said Stoick, taking Hiccup by the shoulders and looking into his eyes, 'is *one thing*. Repeat after me: KEEP KICKING!'

'Keep kicking,' said Hiccup slowly.

'LOUDER!' bellowed Stoick, punching the air.

'KEEP KICKING!' shouted Hiccup, punching the air too.

'That's the spirit!' beamed Stoick. 'I know you'll make me proud, so don't let me down, now!' And he marched off, beaming happily.

Both Old Wrinkly and Hiccup sighed as they watched Stoick bustling off.

'He's a good lad Stoick, really,' wheezed Old Wrinkly, 'but he never EVER listens.'

'No,' agreed Hiccup sadly, 'he doesn't. I haven't got a HOPE of beating Snotlout.'

Old Wrinkly turned his bright, razor-shell-sharp eyes on his grandson. 'We'll see,' said Old Wrinkly. 'Now, this is very important, Hiccup. *Have you got your ticking-thing?*'

'Yes,' answered Hiccup, surprised.

The ticking-thing was a strange round object, with a front that was hard and transparent, like ice. Behind it were all these rune numbers set in different circles, and at least seven arrows, all different colours.

Hiccup had discovered many uses for the ticking-thing. One arrow seemed to tell the time. Another always pointed north, which was extremely useful if you were lost. And since it was quite a changeable day, with the prospect of this strong easterly wind blowing you off course, Hiccup thought it might be handy on this occasion. The ticking-thing was waterproof, too.

Hiccup's only worry was that he was going to LOSE it, so he had attached it to his wrist with a long piece of rope, and then tucked it into his waistcoat pocket.

'Excellent!' said Old Wrinkly. 'Hand it to me, for a moment...'

Hiccup took the ticking-thing out from his pocket. Old Wrinkly opened the back of it and began to fiddle with some of the little buttons inside.

'Now, Hiccup,' said Old Wrinkly, 'I haven't got time to explain, but you have to return to this beach within THREE MONTHS, FIVE DAYS AND SIX HOURS, do you understand me?'

'THREE MONTHS, FIVE DAYS, AND SIX HOURS?' gasped Hiccup. 'What ARE you talking about? I'm not going to last more than *fifteen* minutes out there!'

'I've set the alarm for you,' said Old

tick tick tock tick tick tock tick tock tick tock tick tock tick

Hiccup's ticking thing.

Wrinkly, putting the ticking-thing back into Hiccup's waistcoat pocket. 'When you have less than six hours left, it will start to tick louder. And if the alarm goes off, well, then you will know you are too late... DON'T BE LATE now, Hiccup, will you? I'm counting on you, boy...'

And Old Wrinkly hurried off to the Judges' Table, with Hiccup staring after him with his mouth open. 'Mad as a banana,' said Hiccup.

All the competitors were crowded at the start line drawn in the sand twenty metres from the sea, chatting with each other.

Big-Boobied Bertha, the Chief of the Bog-Burglar Tribe, was slapping Blubberwing fat on to her arms, her gigantic boobies flapping so buoyantly and joyously in the wind that it looked as if any second they might carry her up into the sky like a couple of hot air balloons.

Bertha had a foghorn voice with the kind of carrying quality that could be heard several islands away. She was telling everyone within a two-mile radius that SHE was Bertha the Unsinkable, the Archipelago Swimming Champion, and that everybody else might as well go home right now.

Bertha
the
Unsinkable

The Murderous Tribe were passing their swords and axes and spears and hammers from hand to hand in a thoughtful fashion. They reminded Hiccup uncomfortably of a load of hairy cannibals waiting for their dinner.

Madguts the Murderous, the head of the Murderous Tribe, stood with his arm muscles rippling menacingly. Even with a brisk wind blowing, he was reeking like a three-week-old seal corpse. He was a stinking seven-foot giant with unattractive blue-black skull tattoos covering his cheek-bones.

One of the most terrifying things about Madguts was that he never spoke. Nobody quite knew why. Some say he lost his tongue wrestling a Stormdragon with his bare hands. Others said that it was merely a nasty cold caught when a small baby. Who knew the reason, but he had never been known to do more than grunt. His repulsive assistant Gumboil, an unpleasant little pimple of a man, did all the speaking for him.

There were three Judges, one of whom was Hiccup's grandfather, Old Wrinkly, whose job was to mark the timing of the race.

The Chief Judge, a sad, unbelievably wrinkly little Bashem-Oik, cleared his throat and announced in a high quivery voice:

The Judge's Hut

'O Hear Ye, Vikings of the Tribes of the Archipelago! He who is the last to return back to this beach from the moment I blow this trumpet shall be declared the Last Man Back. He must be able to Swear, according to ancient tradition, that he "did not seek aid by Float or Boat". And as a prize for this contest he may make a single demand of the other two Chieftains. Do you Chieftains swear that you will agree to this demand?'

'We swear,' swore Bertha, Stoick and Madguts the Murderous.

Camicazi, Big-Boobied Bertha's tiny tangle-haired daughter, trotted over to wish Hiccup luck. One of the best Burglars in the Archipelago, Camicazi wasn't afraid of anything or anybody.

'Lovely day for a swim, isn't it?' she said cheerily. 'I can't wait to get in the water.'

Around Camicazi's legs curled a beautiful Mood-dragon called the Stormfly. A Mood-dragon, as its name suggests, is a chameleon that changes colour according to its mood, and this particular Mood-dragon was unusual because it not only spoke Dragonese, but also NORSE, the language of the humans.

"hello, loser Toothless" drawled Stormfly

'Hello, Toothless,' drawled the Stormfly, batting her beautiful long eyelashes at him.

Toothless turned bright red.

He had a bit of a crush on the Stormfly and immediately he began to show off, turning cartwheels in the air and blowing complicated smoke rings that went down the wrong way and gave him a coughing fit.

Toothless turned bright red. He had a bit of a crush on the Stormfly.

As they were standing there, Snotlout sneaked up behind them and whisked Gobber's cloak from off poor Fishlegs's shoulders, revealing the armbands for everybody to see.

'Whoops!' grinned Snotlout. 'Silly me!'

'HA HA HA HA HA!' roared the crowd, pointing at Fishlegs and jumping up and down in joy. 'THERE'S A HOOLIGAN OVER HERE WHO'S WEARING *ARMBANDS!*'

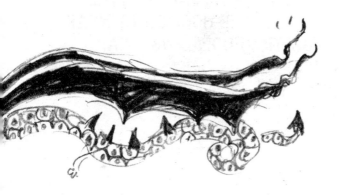

'These aren't armbands!' shouted Hiccup, desperately trying to save the situation. 'They're *weapons*! Inflatable shoulder armour! Very strange and deadly!'

Stoick the Vast blushed purple and swelled up with anger and irritation. That ridiculous fish-legged boy was bringing dishonour on to the Hooligan Tribe.

'Isn't that your SON, Stoick, standing next to the little loser?' grinned Gumboil.

Hiccup was quite a funny sight himself. Covered in shingly sand from head to toe, he resembled nothing so much as a skinny little breadcrumbed kipper ready for the pan.

Stoick tried to stop himself from thinking, *Why does Hiccup always have to make such a spectacle of himself? Why can't he be friends with somebody suitably violent and normal? And why is he covered head to foot in sand?* before yelling loudly and loyally: 'My son is right! The weird little Warrior is wearing the latest in inflatable defence-wear!'

But he was shouted down by the crowd, who were chanting: 'THE HOOLIGANS WEAR ARMBANDS! THE HOOLIGANS WEAR ARMBANDS!'

And then to Stoick's intense relief:

PPPPPPPAAAAAAAAARRRRRP! went the
horn to announce the start of the race, and the Viking
Warriors forgot about teasing the Hooligans, and the
crowd went wild as the Viking Warriors stampeded
through the wind and into the water like a herd of
runaway buffalo, plaits flying, bellies wobbling.

'GO, BOG-BURGLARS GO!'

'UP THE MURDEROUS!'

'HOOLIGANS HURRAH!'

Snotlout sprinted through the shallows, flexing
his muscles and waving to the crowd, before making a
fancy swallow dive into the slightly deeper water and
setting off in a horribly efficient crawl.

Stoick tried hard to control his temper, and keep
the disappointment out of his voice as he walked over
to Hiccup and reproved his son sternly, 'You are a
Warrior-in-Training now, Hiccup, and this is NOT the
moment to be playing in the sand.'

'But I'm not!' protested
Hiccup. 'I'm just covered
in sand because…
because…'

… but Stoick
had already stalked
off.

HA! HA! HA! HA! H

'Oh, jumping jellyfish!' exclaimed
Fishlegs, in a wriggle of anxiety. 'I can't see a THING
through these glasses now!'

The Blubberwing goo Snotlout had poured over
Fishlegs's head had so attached itself to
the glass that it was indeed like trying
to peer through a dense pea-green
fog. Poor Fishlegs staggered forward,
in completely the OPPOSITE
direction to the ocean.

'Hang on,' grinned Camicazi,
'isn't the sea the other way?'

'Fishlegs!' hissed Hiccup
anxiously. 'You're going
the wrong way!'

The
crowd was
divided
between cheering on the
Warriors and laughing at the
sight of the only three who hadn't set
off yet, which were Hiccup, Fishlegs and Camicazi.

Ooooh...
where am
I going?

Fishlegs was running increasingly fast in
completely the opposite direction to the ocean,

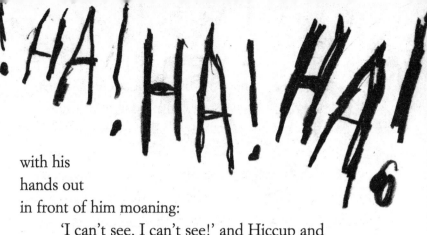

!HA! HA! HA!

with his
hands out
in front of him moaning:

'I can't see, I can't see!' and Hiccup and
Camicazi were running after him, saying:
'It's this way, Fishlegs, this way!'

So: 'HA HA HA HA HA!' yelled the watching
crowd, parting to let poor blind Fishlegs blunder on
up the beach.

Eventually Hiccup caught up with Fishlegs,
who tripped over somebody's discarded trousers,
and with the help of Camicazi he managed to
steer his friend back
in the direction of
the ocean.

And such was
Hiccup's embarrassment
at the whole situation,
that he was almost
RELIEVED to

this is SO embarrassing

enter the breath-quenching, chest-burning chill of the water.

Hiccup was so busy with the humiliation of this moment that he did not realise what had happened to his father and Big-Boobied Bertha.

What had happened was this. Stoick the Vast, Big-Boobied Bertha and Madguts the Murderous swaggered out into the surf in a more leisurely way. All three of them were certain they would win. Stoick forgot about his disappointment with his son as he remembered something amusing.

'Tell you what, Bertha,' whispered Stoick, giving Bertha a friendly poke on the shoulder, 'let's agree, *whichever* of us wins, we teach that Madguts a lesson. We'll get him to row across the Sullen Sea in a bathtub, with his underpants on his head!'

Big-Boobied Bertha roared with laughter until the tears ran down her hairy cheeks. 'For once in your life, Stoick, you old warthog,' she bellowed, 'you've had a good idea! It's a plan, then...'

When they were just entering the water, Madguts
grunted at Gumboil, his eye alight with sneakiness,
and Gumboil said craftily, 'Madguts can't help
but notice that you're wearing that old-fashioned
BLUBBERWING FAT… it doesn't keep out the
cold half as well as the Deepest Purple Fleshfang Oil
that Madguts is wearing… you put this on and you're
never cold again. Lasts until next winter.'

'Oh Toenail Clippings of Thor!' exclaimed
Bertha, staring down at her luminous green body
in disappointment. 'I thought I'd got the very latest
thing!'

Stoick gazed at Madguts's glowing violet chest in admiration and envy. Madguts was so warm under his coating of Deepest Purple Fleshfang Oil that a light steam was rising off his tattooed chest and blowing away in the wind.

'Madguts wants this to be a fair fight,' smiled Gumboil silkily. 'Why don't you try some of his stuff, to make it all equal? We've left the pot just behind you at the edge of the water… we didn't need it any more, because just the one application is sufficient…'

'Well that's mighty kind of you, Madguts!' beamed Stoick. 'But hang on, can we go back there? Hasn't the Race already started?'

Gumboil waved the thought away with one airy hand. 'Oh no…' he reassured the Chieftains cheerily, 'no, the Race doesn't start until you actually start swimming… didn't you know that?'

Stoick and Big-Boobied Bertha said, 'Ah, yes, of course,' and nodded wisely as if they had really known that all along, and turned back and waded out of the sea to pick up the little black pot of Fleshfang Oil that was sitting just a couple of feet beyond the water's edge…

'That trickster Madguts!' said Stoick, tut-tutting in mild disgust. 'Fair fight indeed! *Look!* There's absolutely nothing left!'

Nor there was, just the merest little purple smear at the very bottom, hardly enough to cover Stoick's big toe.

It turned out that that wasn't the *only* thing Madguts had been tricky about.

Stoick looked up as he realised that all around him the crowd was gasping in astonishment and disappointment. The Hooligans, in particular, were wrenching their beards in dismay. And standing right in front of Stoick and Big-Boobied Bertha was the Chief Judge, looking more depressed than ever, his spectacles perched on the end of his nose.

'Commiserations,' said the Chief Judge, gloomily scratching their names down on the parchment in front of him. 'YOU are the First Man (and Woman) back. A dead heat. How do you spell Bertha?'

Stoick laughed and patted the Chief Judge on the head. 'Oh no! Oh *no*, my good little Oik, I think you do not understand the rules. The Race doesn't start until you actually start *swimming…*'

'Of course I understand the rules,' said the Chief Judge calmly. 'I am the *Judge*. If you get out of the water, you've ended the race.'

'But… but… but… of course we're going back

IN again!' spluttered Big-Boobied Bertha in horror.

'Oh, no, you're not,' said the Chief Judge. 'My decision is final.'

Stoick and Big-Boobied Bertha looked like they were going to explode.

'Old Wrinkly!' gasped Stoick. 'Tell him! We can't possibly have LOST the Race!'

Old Wrinkly surveyed the twenty sand-timers in front of him. 'I'm afraid you have,' he said sadly. 'And in three minutes twenty-two seconds exactly. A new Competition Record.'

'But *I'm* the Archipelago Swimming Champion!' shouted Big-Boobied Bertha, raising her great fist in the air. 'Bertha the Unsinkable!'

'AND MADGUTS THE MURDEROUS SAID IT WOULD BE FINE!' yelled Stoick. Even as he said the words, it finally dawned on Stoick and Big-Boobied Bertha (who were not the brightest Chieftains on the block) that they had been taken for a ride.

Two minutes before, Bertha and Stoick had been strutting on the sand, all proud and puffed up like a couple of fat cockerels, so certain had they been of victory.

Now they deflated like the air leaking out of a couple of large and handsome balloons. Bertha's boobies drooped, Stoick's magnificent biceps sagged.

'That rotten, low-down, cheating, Murderous stink-pot!' said Stoick from between gritted teeth. 'He's only gone and tricked us into losing the race!'

3. ISN'T THAT SNOTLOUT A LOVELY GUY?

Hiccup and Fishlegs and Camicazi didn't see what was happening behind them.

They had some problems of their own.

Hiccup had set off as fast as he possibly could, still hot with embarrassment at the scene on the beach.

'Wait up,' begged Fishlegs, sploshing after Hiccup and Camicazi in a clumsy dog-paddle,

'it's really tricky trying to swim in these beastly armbands. We don't have to go *too* far you know, we're not Warriors, we're only in this competition for the fun of it... always supposing your idea of fun is freezing your horns off in Sharkworm-infested waters, of course...'

As soon as Hiccup got out of his depth, the weight of his helmet and his sword made him drop abruptly, and it was only by kicking madly that he was able to keep his chin out of the water.

Even Camicazi was finding that swimming fully armed took a lot of concentration. Her sword and daggers weighed her down so far to the right that she had a tendency to swim round in circles.

'Oh BOTHER!' complained Hiccup. 'How am I possibly going to beat Snotlout at this rate?'

They were so busy trying to keep afloat that they hadn't noticed Snotlout and Dogsbreath the Duhbrain swimming up behind them. (Which shows how distracted they were – Dogsbreath's splashy crawl was as noisy as a hippo in a bathtub.)

The two bullies overheard the last bit of the conversation, and Snotlout was laughing so hard he was in danger of drowning. 'You said it, Hiccup, you loser!' crowed Snotlout.

'One of *you* three? Beat *me*? I've never heard anything so funny in my life!'

'Her Her Her,' grunted Dogsbreath, snorting seawater out of his nose.

'The thing is, Hiccup,' sneered Snotlout, 'you heard everybody laughing on the beach… you guys are just an embarrassment to the Tribe.'

Snotlout's eyes were alight with real murderous malice. He looked over his shoulder to check that nobody could see what he was doing. 'I am now going to give *you*, Hiccup, a lesson in being a Viking Hero, and *you*, Fishlegs, a lesson in how to swim without your armbands on…'

One of You three? Beat ME???

'No!'
shrieked Fishlegs,
trying to swim away.

But he hadn't a hope of escaping.

Both Snotlout and Dogsbreath were
big, burly adolescents and they caught him easily,
ducking Hiccup and Camicazi along the way. Snotlout
popped the right armband with his dagger and
Dogsbreath removed the left.

'Now, Hiccup,' purred Snotlout. 'You can just
about make it back to shore on your own, but if
you try to do it holding Fishlegs, I don't fancy your
chances. So… what do you do? I suggest you do us all
a favour, and ditch the LOSER, but it's up to you,
of course.'

And the two bullies swam away, laughing.

Hiccup resurfaced,
gasping, and thrashed
through the water towards
poor Fishlegs, who was going
under for the second time. With the help of Toothless,
Stormfly and Fishlegs's hunting-dragon Horrorcow, he
got the boy upright with his head out of the water, but
Fishlegs was so terrified he was struggling and in danger
of dragging Hiccup under with him.

'STOP PANICKING AND RELAX!' shouted
Hiccup sharply.

'RELAX!' shrieked Fishlegs. 'HOW CAN I
RELAX? *I'M DROWNING! DROWNING ISN'T
VERY RELAXING!*

But he stopped struggling, and forced himself to
go limp, and floated on to the surface with Hiccup and
Camicazi holding him by the shoulders.

'OK,' said Hiccup, in his I'm-trying-to-stay-calm-
but-really-I-want-to-run-around-in-circles-screaming voice,

'*now* I think we might have a bit of a problem...'

As Hiccup bobbed upwards on the waves, he could see the shoreline, and suddenly it seemed very distant. Hiccup wasn't sure that he could make that swim back carrying Fishlegs all the way, even with Camicazi helping.

This is the trouble with a Proper Viking Swimming Race. It's a game of judgment as well as endurance. You have to be very careful that you don't go out so far that you run out of energy to make it back.

'We'd better get Fishlegs back to the shore, then,' Hiccup said with a confidence he was far from feeling.

'Carrot, anyone?' smiled Horrorcow, sensing a crisis and swooping down from above in a motherly way. 'It will help keep your strength up for the swim...'

'Not now, Horrorcow,' said Hiccup, and then (trying to sound extra casual), 'Horrorcow, maybe you should just flap back to the shore and tell them to send out some Rescue Dragons for us...'

'Righti-ho,' replied Horrorcow cheerily, and she flapped off. 'Keep kicking...'

'Keep kicking... keep kicking... keep kicking...'

Hiccup lost count of the amount of times he said this in the next half hour.

For a strange thing was happening. The more they kicked, the FURTHER they seemed to be getting from the beach. During the confrontation with Snotlout and Dogsbreath, they had drifted into a tide that was carrying them out to sea.

They could no longer hear the friendly shouts of other Vikings. Apart from the sound of their own splashing, they were alone. Alone in a stone-cold sea that stretched out for miles around them.

'I'm getting tired,' said Camicazi, who was never tired.

It is a little difficult to see how their situation could get any worse.

But that, as anybody who has read Hiccup's memoirs before will know, is often a sign that things are going to get REALLY, REALLY bad.

Suddenly Toothless, who had been fishing for mackerel, shot shrieking out of the sea only centimetres from Hiccup's ear.

'What is it, Toothless?' gasped Hiccup, as the little dragon hovered above him.

'S-s-s-something n-n-nasty...' stammered Toothless, spiralling upwards on shaking wings, 'something nasty down there!'

'What sort of nasty?' swallowed Hiccup.

'Toothless not know...' replied Toothless. 'NASTY sort of n-n nasty... didn't wait and see... something b-b-black...'

'What's wrong?' shivered Fishlegs. 'What's he saying?'

Is Something
N-N-NASTY!
Down there
in the
water!

'Oh,
nothing,' lied
Hiccup carelessly.
'You know Toothless,
he's easily spooked... *Keep
kicking, keep kicking,*' whispered Hiccup, looking all
around him, 'but kick *softly...*'

'Why softly?' squeaked Fishlegs, beginning to
panic and sinking as a result. 'There is something,
isn't there? What is it? DARKBREATHERS?
SHARKWORMS? TERRORFANGS????'

'It's nothing,' whispered Hiccup soothingly, 'you
just concentrate on floating, Fishlegs...'

Then, suddenly Camicazi let out a
piercing scream.

'AAAAGHHHH!'

She thrashed around
in the water for a second,
and then she was
dragged underneath by
some unknown force.

'*Camicazi!*' shrieked Hiccup, trying to hold up Fishlegs and look underneath the water at the same time. '*Camicazi! Camicazi!!!!*'

But she was gone.

4. A REALLY, *REALLY* BAD SITUATION

'Oh for Thor's sake, oh for Thor's sake...' cried Hiccup, looking desperately around him. But there was no sign of Camicazi.

Just the silent mists, and below them... why, below them, there could be ANYTHING down there in the water. It could be Darkbreathers, that liked to drag their victims underneath the water and suck out their blood. It could be Sharkworms, that killed with their foot-long fangs, or grabbed a take-away of a dangling limb, and swam on.

'*Where is she? Where is she? Where is she?*' Fishlegs kept repeating, as if Hiccup knew the answer.

One terrified minute passed.

And then Fishlegs, too, screamed, and was dragged under, out of Hiccup's arms.

'*Fishlegs!*' yelled Hiccup.

Hiccup was alone in the cold grey ocean.

Never had his poor flapping feet felt so vulnerable.

There was nothing he could do. He could not run, or fly away (although Toothless was valiantly trying to haul him out of the water by the back of his waistcoat).

And then he felt the first searching nibble on his ankle…

Hiccup screamed, and tried, clumsily, to splash forward.

But whatever-it-was took a firm grip on his leg and pulled him underwater.

Hiccup just had time to take a big lungful of air. The water around him turned swiftly from green to grey to black as he was dragged down into the sea.

So this is it… thought Hiccup… as he went deeper still… *This is what it is like to die…*

Just as his lungs were about to burst, he was pulled back the other way up, the water turned from black to grey to green to white again, and he was hauled out of the sea and into the sky.

Hiccup was being carried upside-down through the air by a gigantic dragon, with a wingspan of about seven metres.

All around him, with great
rasping shrieks, a whole pack of the
creatures was leaping out
of the sea, shooting
upwards as if they
were arrows being shot
out of Neptune's bow.

The dragon holding
Hiccup was flying so low
that Hiccup's fingers were
scraping the surface of the
water. It swung him
upwards as
if he were
a piece of
mackerel and let
him go, sending Hiccup
cartwheeling through the
air, and as he was JUST
about to hit the sea, another
dragon dived and caught him,
this time by the arms.

Out of the corner of his eye, Hiccup
could see Fishlegs and Camicazi being carried
by other dragons in the pack in a similar fashion.

He tipped his head upwards
to try and see what had captured
them. It was Raptortongues.

Raptortongues are most peculiar.
They look like perfectly normal dragons that
have been accidentally stepped on by a giant,
and squashed flat as a pancake. They are often
used by Vikings to spy on enemy Tribes, because
they can fly low and swift and silent over enemy
territory without anyone realising they are there.

Raptortongues

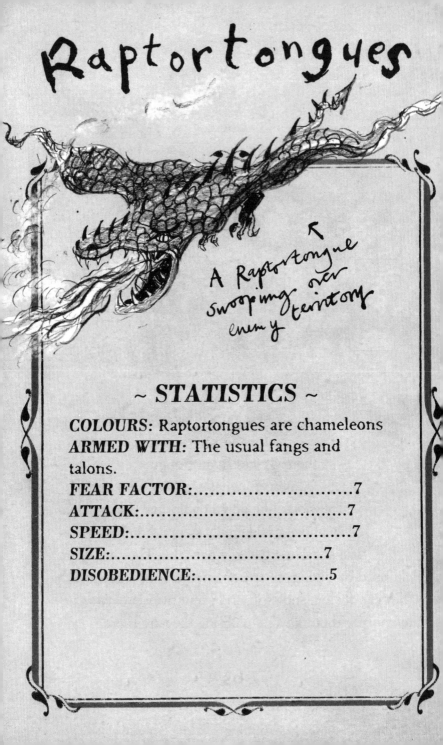

A Raptortongue swooping over enemy territory

~ STATISTICS ~

COLOURS: Raptortongues are chameleons

ARMED WITH: The usual fangs and talons.

FEAR FACTOR:....................................7

ATTACK:..7

SPEED:..7

SIZE:...7

DISOBEDIENCE:.............................5

Raptortongues live hidden in the deep crevasses of the Murderous Mountains or the Gorge of the Thunderbolt of Thor. They have an extraordinary ability to flatten themselves, which means they can squeeze through surprisingly small spaces. They make excellent spy dragons.

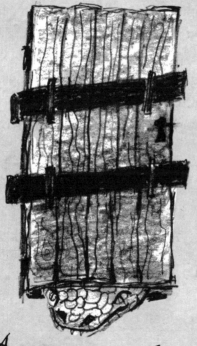

A young Raptortongue squeezing under a locked door.

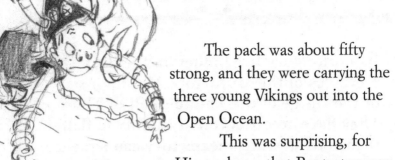

The pack was about fifty strong, and they were carrying the three young Vikings out into the Open Ocean.

This was surprising, for Hiccup knew that Raptortongues were Archipelago dragons, not Ocean creatures at all. WHERE, for Thor's sake, were they taking them? The Raptortongues flew on and on. Every now and then, when Hiccup's arms were aching so hard he thought they would pull out of their sockets, the Raptortongues would fling him upside-down again.

Hiccup attempted to talk to the Raptortongue who was carrying him, but it merely adjusted

its grip, and snapped, 'You say one more word, and I will remove your head.'

Hiccup was an intelligent boy, and he judged that it might be wiser to shut up.

Eventually a smudge appeared on the horizon, gradually growing bigger and bigger as they drew nearer. At first Hiccup thought it was an island with a volcano on it, for it was belching out a thick grey-green smoke. But as they grew nearer and nearer Hiccup realised it wasn't an island at all, but a boat.

And what a boat it was.

Steam Balloon

The Keep-the Boat-From Sinking and Scare Away the Seadragons Big Machine

cages

chimney

slave hatch

landing boats

Norbert's tent

Flying Machine

The American Dream II

Hiccup had never seen anything like it before, and Hiccup had seen plenty of boats in his life. Hooligan raiding ships, Bog-Burglar sneak-boats, Roman Dragon-Rustling Galleons, Uglithug Slaving Craft... you name it, Hiccup had seen it.

But *this* was something completely different.

It was truly immense. It was about six times the size and depth of an ordinary Viking ship. It had not one, but *two* masts. And planted right at the back of the deck was a strange gigantic tube like a bent chimney, out of which the smoke was curling.

Perhaps this was a ghost ship, or Hiccup had stumbled into sleep and this was all merely some weird nightmare.

The Raptortongues approached it through the great drifts of smoke, and circled the gigantic vessel twice before they landed, swooping low over the prow of the ship.

UH-OH-UH-OH-UH-OH, thought Hiccup in an agony of coughing as the Raptortongue folded back his wings, preparing to land on deck. *UH-OH-UH-OH-UH-OH-UH-OH...*

The ship's deck was thronged with a particularly unpleasant load of barbarians, who let out a cheer as the Raptortongue let Hiccup go, and laughed wildly as

he sprawled on the deck, with Camicazi and Fishlegs
being dropped beside him.

'COME BACK AND FIGHT LIKE *VIKINGS,*
YOU COWARDLY BATS!' shrieked Camicazi, in a
twist of fury at being kidnapped by the Raptortongues,
and their new captors only laughed the more.

The young Vikings were wound around with ropes
as securely as chickens trussed up for slaughter and tied
upside-down to the central mast of the ship.

Even Toothless and the Stormfly had been
captured, and tied up next to their Masters.

So the mood of the three young Heroes was
gloomy, anxious, even terrified. They didn't know what
their captors were going to do to them.

What was a VERY bad sign, however, was that
the entire crew was chanting, 'KILL, KILL, KILL,
KILL, KILL! *KILL* THE CHILDREN, KILL,
KILL, *KILL!*'

Even Camicazi, who liked to look on the bright
side, could tell that this didn't look promising.

'Do you think they're talking about US?'
whimpered Fishlegs.

'Well, we're the only children *here*, aren't we?'
Hiccup pointed out, teeth chattering together like
crabs' claws.

'We should probably be planning our escape,' chirped Camicazi, cheerily listening to the cruel laughter and jeering of the brutes, who were now merrily lobbing fish at the poor captives.

'You're right, Camicazi,' admitted Hiccup, 'but it looks like there are at least two hundred of them... They're heavily armed... and I don't know about you, but at the moment *I* am dripping wet, unarmed, and tied securely upside-down to a mast. I'm not sure *how* we're going to escape from this position. I guess we could try reasoning with them, but they don't look all that reasonable to me.'

"LET US GO, YOU PLANKTON HEARTED, JELLYFISH MUSCLED SLIMY SONS OF SHRIMPS! OR I'LL GRIND YOUR BONES TO SAND AND THROW YOU BACK IN TO THE SEA WITH THE EELS WHERE YOU BELONG! YOU CAN'T KEEP A BOG-BURGLAR UNDER ROPE AND CHAINS!"

... shouted Camacazi.

The growling and chanting increased to double the volume, and the air rained down with fish thrown in their direction.

Shouts of, 'You and whose army, blondie?'

'Nice reasoning, Camicazi,' said Hiccup.

One of the barbarians strolled over to a tent built in the centre of the ship and shouted, 'Bo-o-o-o-ossss! They're he-e-ere!'

'It appears,' said Hiccup grimly, 'that we're expected. That's not a good sign.'

'NONE of this is a good sign!' shivered Fishlegs. 'Who do you think has kidnapped us?'

Hiccup wracked his brains. Who hadn't been at the Friendly Inter-Tribe Swimming Race? Bashem-Oiks? Uglithugs?

'I *do* hope it's not Uglithugs,' whimpered Fishlegs.

But it was much worse than Uglithugs. For the barbarian shipmates drew back the curtains on the tent in the middle of the ship, and there, sitting having a little light supper together, were three men who were three strokes of Very Bad Luck Indeed.

Reading from left to right, they were Madguts the Murderous, Norbert the Nutjob, Chief of the Hysteric Tribe, and Gumboil, Madguts's lovely assistant.

5. AN UNPLEASANT OLD ACQUAINTANCE

They were sharing a deer between them, and Norbert and Madguts made a disgusting sight, sitting there with their hands dipped scarlet in blood as they tore the poor thing limb from limb.

Gumboil was a little more delicate in his manners, and he was nibbling daintily at a piece of deer liver on the end of a long pointed black fork.

Norbert the Nutjob swallowed the last bits of wine that he was drinking out of a skull, chucked some fleshy bits of deer over his shoulder, and rubbed his bloody hands on his shirtfront.

'Oh well done, Madguts old chap,' said Norbert enthusiastically, 'your Raptortongues have brought us the victims.'

Hiccup didn't like the sound of the word 'victim'. 'What's going on?' he stammered.

'Why have you brought us here? We need to get back to our Swimming Race... And why is Madguts here? He's supposed to be in the Swimming Race too...'

Norbert got up and

thrust his face into Hiccup's face. One mad
eyeball stared straight at Hiccup, red veins
bulging all over it like lines on a lunatic
map, a violent tic sending the pupil
quivering and trembling in a wild dance
of rage.

'*Your* race is over,' said Norbert
with satisfaction. 'Madguts and
I have made a little agreement.
Madguts has brought me YOU,
and I, in return, have put him up
on my ship here for a couple
of hours. He will then swim
back to shore well after the
others, making sure that
HE is the Last Man
Back...'

'But that's *cheating*!'
protested Hiccup. 'You're not
supposed to seek aid by Float
or Boat!'

'*Of course* it's cheating!'
laughed Norbert. 'You think
your ancestor, Grimbeard the
Ghastly, didn't cheat long ago
in that famous Swimming
Race when he became King
of the Archipelago? It
isn't physically possible
to carry on swimming
for THREE WHOLE
MONTHS...'

tick
tock
tick
tock

tick
t

tick
t

'That *is* a long time,' grinned Gumboil. 'I'm sorry to interrupt, but we'll be off now, since you've got what you wanted, Norbert. Madguts has rested enough, and he has a race to come last in.'

Madguts the Murderous grunted and wiped his bloody palms on the front of his waistcoat. He shook Norbert the Nutjob by the hand, and did a few leg stretches, before swallow-diving off the edge of the boat, followed by the repulsive Gumboil, holding his nose and doing a bomb. The Raptortongues unfolded their bat-like wings and followed them.

'Well, well, well, if it isn't the weird little red-haired boy,' smiled Norbert the Nutjob. 'When last we met, I seem to remember that you stole my ticking-thing, burned down my Great Hall, chewed off my moustaches, and fed Papa to the Squealers.'*

'That was an accident!' protested Hiccup. 'An unfortunate SERIES of accidents which we deeply regret, don't we guys?'

'Mmff,' snorted Norbert. 'Didn't I warn you that the next time we bumped into each other I would KILL you?'

'Well, *lovely* as it is to see you again,' said Hiccup tactfully (you should always be polite to madmen carrying axes), 'I didn't exactly PLAN this meeting...'

---

*See *How to Cheat a Dragon's Curse*.

'My Chopper has been *aching* to bite your head off ever since...' Norbert lovingly stroked the double-headed axe that he carried with him everywhere. One side of the axe was bright and shining gold, the other a blackened twisted mass of rotting metal. 'And you guys too, of course.' He generously included Camicazi and Fishlegs, in case they were feeling left out. 'But I can't quite decide whether to kill you right now, or take you on our little expedition and THEN kill you... dear oh dear... life is full of tough decisions...'

'KILL THEM NOW! KILL THEM NOW!' shouted the watching Hysterical crew gleefully.

'Expedition?' said Hiccup, his heart sinking lower still. 'What do you mean *expedition*? Where are you going?'

'Oh… not far…' Norbert the Nutjob gave a peculiarly nasty grin. 'Just a little light sailing, to try out my new boat… I thought we might drop in on AMERICA, you know…'

'But there's no such place as America!' objected Fishlegs. 'The world is as flat as a pancake and if you sail too far to the west you fall off the end of it!'

'SHUDDUPPPPP!!!' roared Norbert, a fanatical gleam in his mad eye. 'The world is round as an orange, and I know there's such a place as America because I've BEEN THERE! I shall return in GLORY, with WARRIORS and MIGHT, and I shall found a great EMPIRE! Just picture me, Norbert the Great, Emperor of the New World!'

Hiccup *was* picturing it. It was a horrible thought.

'I shall call this new country *Nutjob-Land*,' said Norbert with satisfaction, making a grand gesture with his axe. 'But in order to get to America in the first place,' Norbert continued, 'I need that ticking-thing that you stole from me the last time we met. Only *that* can show us the way. So… which of you has it?'

He jabbed his axe at them, one at a time.

'Is it the funny-looking kid with the red hair and the freckles… the little blonde lunatic… or the boy with a face like a fish?'

83

The Axe of DOOM will decide!

'It's *me*, Hiccup Horrendous Haddock the Third,' said Hiccup, 'and you're standing on it right now.'

Hiccup was hanging upside-down, so the ticking-thing had fallen out of his pocket, and it was now lying on the deck with Norbert's great big maniac foot on it.

'My ticking-thing!' cried Norbert delightedly, untying it from Hiccup's wrist and clasping it to his chest.

'And now, Hiccup,' smiled Norbert, reminding Hiccup that he had more important things to be thinking of by pressing the blackened edge of his two-headed axe against Hiccup's throat, 'as I said, I can't quite decide whether to kill you now, or once we get to America... understand?'

'Perfectly...' gulped Hiccup.

'The Axe of DOO-OO-OOM will decide!' roared Norbert, throwing wide his arms. (Wild cheers and stampings of feet from the bloodthirsty crowd.) 'I shall throw it up in the air, and if it lands gold side down, you come with us to America. But if it lands black side down... why, if it lands *black* side down you *die on the spot*!' yelled Norbert the Nutjob. 'How lucky are you feeling today, Hiccup Horrendous Haddock the Third?'

'Well I've been thinking about that,' muttered Hiccup, 'and so far I reckon this has been just about the unluckiest day I've had in *years*.'

'Oh goodee,' grinned Norbert the Nutjob, 'I HATE waiting for my treats.'

'THROW THE AXE! THROW THE AXE! THROW THE AXE!' yelled the Hysterics joyously.

'DEATH OR AMERICA!' shouted Norbert the Nutjob.

'DEATH OR AMERICA!' screamed the Hysterics back at him.

'Death or America,' groaned Hiccup, Fishlegs and Camicazi.

Hiccup closed his eyes as with a manic scream Norbert the Nutjob threw the great axe high, high in the air.

The Hysterics scattered in all directions.

The axe swooped upwards, turning over and over, first the gold side up, then the black... up and up it soared...

And then it seemed to hover for a moment before it began the plunge downward towards the deck. Was it the gold side down or was it the black?

Hiccup squinted anxiously through his salty strands of hair, trying to see.

'It's the black! It's the black!' shouted Norbert the Nutjob with mad glee. 'Prepare to die!'

And with horror Hiccup realised it WAS the black side plunging towards the deck. And there was absolutely NOTHING he could do about it.

6. THE AXE OF DOOM DECIDES

Hiccup's mind raced desperately.

He couldn't move, but inspiration suddenly struck...

'CAN YOU *READ* THE TICKING-THING, NORBERT?' screamed Hiccup.

Norbert looked at the ticking-thing... *Curses!*...
He couldn't...

Curses.
He couldn't.

... but the axe was steaming towards the deck of the ship, and the Axe of Doom was never allowed to be wrong... So Norbert the Nutjob gave Verociously Violent a big shove so that Verociously got in between the axe and the deck, getting a nasty scratch on his arm in the process.

'NOW LOOK WHAT YOU MADE ME DO!' roared Norbert the Nutjob. 'OK, untie the wretched little burglars!'

Muttering with disappointed bloodlust, the Hysterics unwound the ropes tying Hiccup, Fishlegs and Camicazi, who fell on to the deck, deeply relieved to be the right way up again, but very dizzy.

'Follow me,' barked Norbert the Nutjob.

Hiccup followed Norbert to the central tent in the middle of the deck.

This tent was Norbert's cabin. Now, Vikings normally travelled very light on board ship. And they didn't generally have cabins at all, just maybe a couple of upturned landing-boats to shield them from the wildness of the wind.

But Norbert was intending to sail to America FOR EVER, so he had packed this ship with every possible thing that a Future Emperor might need over there in a New World. Tables, chairs, chessboards, smashsticks-on-ice sticks, bashyballs, skis.

The walls of this tent-cabin of his were covered with crazy drawings of Norbert's latest inventions, and also with maps. Norbert jabbed a fat finger at one particular map with some little squiggly numbers drawn on it.

'THIS was the Map my father Bigjob used to go to America,' said Norbert.

Here is what

The funny round TICKING THING can DO:

This arrow here always points to the NORTH

These arrows tell the time.

Hiccup doesn't yet know what the question mark and the Lightning arrows do.

This arrow tells you how far to go EAST

This arrow tells you how far to go WEST

This arrow is a LIE DETECTOR

Tell a lie when you are holding the ticking-thing and it whirls round and round crazily.

'He read those funny little numbers, and he checked the ticking-thing, and that would tell him which way to go.'

Norbert handed Hiccup the map and the ticking-thing. There were nine arrows on the dial.

The two little ordinary arrows told the time much

more accurately than Old Wrinkly's complicated candlesticks. The little fat arrow always pointed to the north, like the North Star. The one with the round circle on the end was a lie detector. Hiccup didn't yet know what the one shaped like a question mark did, or the funny little jagged one like a piece of lightning.

But the remaining two told him how far to go upwards, and how far to go westwards.*

He sat there staring back and forth from the ticking-thing to the Map for such a long time that Norbert grew impatient, and roared:

'HURRY UP BOY, HURRY UP! We haven't got all DAY!'

'The quickest way to America, if such a place really exists, is in *that* direction.' Hiccup pointed over towards some distant storm-clouds to the north. 'But we'd have to go through the Ice Islands and there are some really unpleasant Ice-Dragons we could meet that way—'

---

*This suggests that the ticking-thing contains a device for calculating LONGTITUDE (what Hiccup describes as 'going westwards'). It was previously thought that the first device for predicting longtitude was the chronometer created in 1773, but Hiccup's memoirs show otherwise.

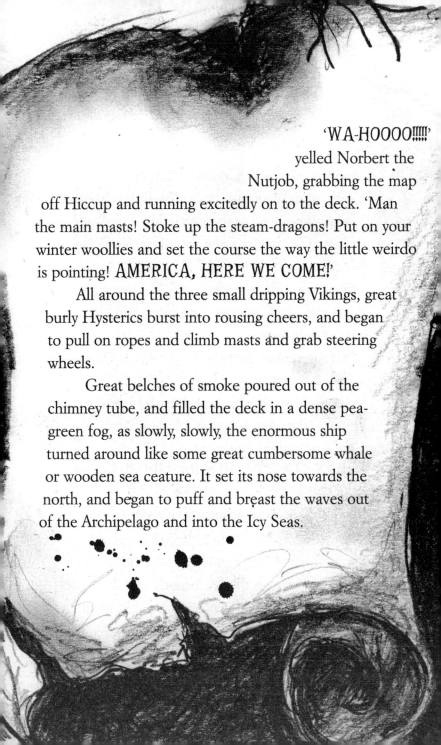

'WA-HOOOO!!!!!'
yelled Norbert the
Nutjob, grabbing the map
off Hiccup and running excitedly on to the deck. 'Man
the main masts! Stoke up the steam-dragons! Put on your
winter woollies and set the course the way the little weirdo
is pointing! AMERICA, HERE WE COME!'

All around the three small dripping Vikings, great
burly Hysterics burst into rousing cheers, and began
to pull on ropes and climb masts and grab steering
wheels.

Great belches of smoke poured out of the
chimney tube, and filled the deck in a dense pea-
green fog, as slowly, slowly, the enormous ship
turned around like some great cumbersome whale
or wooden sea ceature. It set its nose towards the
north, and began to puff and breast the waves out
of the Archipelago and into the Icy Seas.

The Land of the sea serpents
BEWARE

AMERICA
this way

The Murderous
Mountains

the DARK SIDE of THE AXE
(a moving little lullaby)

Come and dance the Deathwalk
Beneath the grinning moon...
We'll do the dance together
In the dying afternoon...

The Deathwalk looks so tricky,
But I think you'll learn it quick,
Just step into my Axe's arms,
She'll teach you in a tick...

See the jolly skeletons
A dancing on the seal
They haven't got no cares how
Not like you and me...
They went and did the
DEATHWALK
That crazy night-time
beat...

And now they partner ghosts and whales
On bony pearly feet...

7. THE QUEST TO DISCOVER AMERICA

So this was how Hiccup, Camicazi and Fishlegs got themselves kidnapped by Norbert the Nutjob, and found themselves in a boat that was sailing out of the Archipelago, never to return.

Of course, Hiccup, Camicazi and Fishlegs did not want to go to America. Besides which, there was the tiny problem of crossing the Great West Ocean which, Hiccup knew, was full of Sea-Dragons so large and fearsome that they could swallow the ship they were standing on in one gulp.

'So... what do we do *now* then, Hiccup?' asked Fishlegs slowly.

'Well,' said Hiccup, through chattering teeth. 'Let's dry our wet things, first of all.'

The chimney at the back of the deck out of which the smoke was pouring was hot to the touch, so they leant against it for a couple of hours, letting the lovely warmth penetrate their frozen bodies. The green streaky remains of the Fleshfang oil on their cheeks and arms made them look like three cold-blooded little lizards baking in the sunshine. Their salty clothes were stiff as cardboard, but at least they were dry.

When they had finally stopped shivering, they began to explore their floating prison.

Hysterics are a Tribe of dreamers, lunatics and inventors, so the *American Dream II* was not your ordinary Viking ship.

The steam pouring out of the chimney was a distinctive grey-green, so Hiccup suspected it was dragon-smoke, probably coming from dragons hidden within the belly of the ship. Hiccup would have loved to see by what mechanism this steam powered the boat.*

The dragons weren't the *only* mad thing about this vessel. There was a weird thing with wings sprouting out of the side that a Hysteric called Red Ronald told them was Norbert's attempt at a Flying Machine. Unfortunately it didn't really work yet.

Several times during the day, Norbert ordered three unfortunate members of his crew to try it out, hauling the Machine all the way up to the top of the Mast on ropes, and then launching it from the crow's nest.

It only stayed up in the sky for a couple of minutes, before crashing spectacularly into the Ocean,

---

*Hiccup's memoirs seem to suggest that Norbert had built a steam-ship, many, many centuries before steam was used to power marine craft. Similarly, the artist Leonardo da Vinci drew designs for a helicopter, a trench-digging machine, a deep-sea diving suit, a revolving bridge, a calculator, a hang-glider and a tank, four hundred years before any of these things were 'invented'.

Wind Powered Flying Machine
Fig. F

This one could work.
Get Violent, Goggle Eyes
and Ronald to try out
and see if they can
make it back over
the hill this time. NaNa

Steam-Powered Machine.
Perhaps not this one.

Fig. P

and the crew members had to be rescued, and the Machine mended again.

And then there was an extraordinary Machine with a wheel that the crew took in turns to pedal with their feet, which was attached to a large trumpet-like funnel. It was very difficult to work out what the purpose of this Machine was. At the moment it was Verociously Violent's turn on the Machine, because his arm was still recovering from the gash he had received from the Axe of Doom incident, so he wasn't much good at pulling on ropes and other tasks around the boat at the moment.

Hiccup was so curious about what the Machine did that he approached Verociously to ask what he was doing.

'Oh, this is the Keep-the-Boat-From-Sinking-and-Scare-Away-the-Big-Sea-Creatures Machine,' explained Verociously Violent, stopping pedalling for a second to answer Hiccup's question. 'It stops the boat from sinking and it also scares away the Sea-Monsters, Great Terrorwings, Seadragonus Giganticus Maximus, that sort of thing.'*

'KEEP PEDALLING! KEEP PEDALLING!' screamed Norbert the Nutjob, marching up, and the Hysteric hurriedly resumed, so fast his feet were a blur.

---

*Some of Norbert's inventions were more practical than others, because the line between genius and total loopiness is quite a fine one.

'And *YOU*,' Norbert turned to Hiccup, 'STOP
DISTRACTING THE CREW! If this man here stops
turning this wheel for even *one
second*, the boat will sink,
and we could be attacked
by one of the Ocean
Dragon-Mammoths.'

'Fascinating,'
said Hiccup, very
politely, thinking,
*nutty as an absolute
fruitcake*.

'Is there any
chance,' gulped Fishlegs hopefully as
they walked away, 'that that thing could
work?'

'Yeah, right,' replied Hiccup. 'Like
a revolving tube with a funnel attached
is *really* going to stop a boat from
sinking...'

At the end of the first day of The
Quest to Discover America, the sun
sank in a glorious technicolour display
of pink and gold streaked with red. The
three young Vikings sat and worried...

and worried… and worried. (Actually, *two* of them worried; Camicazi just played with Toothless.)

They worried until it was late at night, and the Hysterics had built a fire on deck, and were singing songs to the rising moon. The songs were about the life of a Viking. You have to imagine Norbert the Nutjob adding the *HO!*s, while banging his axe on the bottom of an iron bucket.

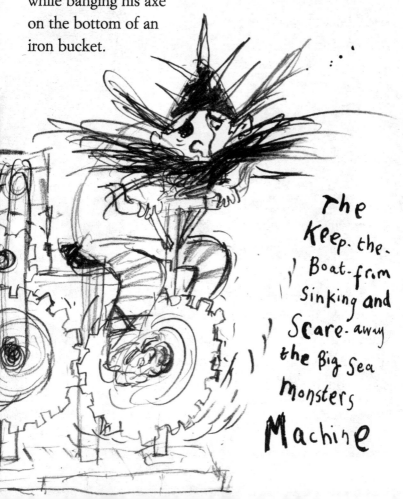

The Keep-the-Boat-from-Sinking and Scare-away-the-Big-Sea-monsters Machine

'We could be safe at
hearth and home
Around a fire with loved ones near
Instead we brave the cold dark wave
The salty kiss of a Hero's grave
Looking for a land we saw…
Once before… long ago…
HO!

Norbert the Nutjob was sitting, a twisted shadow watching the singers, his cabin shrouded close around him. Only his eyes gleamed in the firelight, as he watched and smoked from a long thin pipe that sent a crooked plume of smoke up into the sail billowing above him and on into the night sky.

'We could take the easy way
Stay at home with loved ones dear
But here we are on rocking waves
Sails spread out like dragons' wings...
Lost out in a hurricane...
Looking for a land we saw...
Once before... long ago...
HO!

As the Hysterics sang on in the warm night, Hiccup's eyes began to close.

But they opened again with a start when the deck beneath Hiccup's feet began to vibrate with a new noise. Strange voices were beginning their own song. Weird voices, singing in a language that Hiccup did not understand, the sound of something so Other and unfamiliar that they were as alien as the music of whales or dolphins calling to each other.

104

Voices coming from deep within the belly of the ship.

'What is *that*?' whispered Fishlegs to Hiccup, with round, scared eyes.

Hiccup's heart plummeted.

He suddenly realised what it might be.

'I wonder,' replied Hiccup slowly, 'if this ship is carrying *slaves* on it?'

The Hysterics stopped to listen too. And as they listened the song changed, to something much more sinister. A shiver went slipping down Hiccup's spine like a cold drop of water. You did not have to understand the language the slaves were speaking to understand what they were saying.

Toothless let out a whine of fear, as if he were a spaniel, and covered his ears with his paws.

They were laying a Curse on the ship. A Curse on the voyage. A Curse on every single Viking man, woman or child who was keeping them there, under those decks...

The hairs stood up on the back of Hiccup's neck.

They went right on singing, that fierce terrible Curse, until Norbert strode to the centre of the deck, and struck it with his axe three times, and shouted:

"SHUDDUP! OR I'LL COME DOWN AND DROWN THE LOT OF YOU!!"

And then it was quiet again.

Hiccup lay in the darkness, his heart beating quick. Oh how he longed to be Home...

It was very late when he fell asleep again, the Hysterics still singing:

> 'Glory comes not to the weak
> A treasure land shines out so strong
> We see it clear from far away
> O Great and Brave and Mighty Thor
> I *hope* that that was land I saw
> Once before... long ago...
> *HO!*

The ship sailed on through the moonlit night.

Apart from four crewmen (one steering the boat, one looking after the Steam-Dragons, one keeping lookout, and one laboriously turning Norbert's mad Monster-Scaring Machine), all the human beings aboard the *American Dream II* had fallen asleep now: Hysterics, Hooligans, friends and foes, all.

What none of these little sleeping human beings knew was how tiny they were compared to the vastness of the world they were about to enter. Nothing seemed to have changed on the quiet and peaceful surface of the water… but in fact they had moved out of the safe, shallow seas of the Archipelago, they had crossed an invisible line in the ocean, and they were now sailing over very deep waters indeed.

Waters fathoms and fathoms deep, a sunless, black and watery desert.

But could it be that *something* was about to stir down in the darkness? The unimaginable enormity of the Open Ocean holds such strange and terrible things, things which we cannot even dream of.

If you were a fanciful person, you could imagine that something dreadful was about to happen. Some dragon-giant of the abyss, sleeping all coiled up like an unwoken tornado, was about to gain consciousness and would move inexorably on the little ship puffing its way across the water.

But we are not fanciful people, so we know that cannot be true.

LEARNING TO SPEAK DRAGONESE
TOOTHLESS WANTS A PET

please
please
please
Please

Nee-ah, Toothless, ta NA aea
un sweetie ickle tootsienipper
par un fluff-squees.
No, Toothless, you CANNOT
have a dear little rat for a pet.

Parsk me pappa na likeit.
Because my dad won't be pleased.

Na un moonhowler, oo un deathscuttler plus DOUBLY
DOUBLY na un fangboggle-limb-scrumcher.

Nor a wolf, or a scorpion,
and DEFINITELY
DEFINITELY not a
shark.

*When Toothless is in
a mood he puffs out so
much black smoke you
can hardly see
him*

Yow is a snakenipper
Yellfatter, plus
yow squeezeblood
ist conja da
sniffersludge.
You are a very mean
Master, and your
heart is made out
of bogeys.

8. THE SLAVEMARK

Hiccup was right, the ship *was* carrying slaves.

Hiccup asked Red Ronald about it the next morning, and Ronald said there were one hundred and nineteen slaves being kept in the hold, all of them Northern Wanderers. Wanderers were very fierce and wild, and they detested Vikings.

It made Hiccup shiver to hear the noise of their Cursing, floating up out of a heavily barred Hatch in the centre of the back deck, all day and all night.

Two days passed.

Each morning Hiccup would read the ticking-thing for Norbert in his cabin, and then the three young Heroes spent the rest of the time dreaming of escape as the ship chugged steadily north and the weather grew colder and colder.

There is no more exciting place for a lively young dragon than a ship in full sail.

The two little dragons were now having a *lovely* time, flying through the rigging, getting tangled up in ropes, sliding down the sails, trying to nick things from the Cooking Cabin without getting caught by the Cook, dashing after mice in the hold, chewing the arms off Norbert's shirts and the bottoms out of his shoes, and in the Stormfly's case, flirting with the hunting-dragons who were lined up, very dignified on the mast-head.

But both dragons avoided the Slave Hatch. Every time Toothless passed it, his hackles rose, and he hissed with fear and alarm.

The three young Heroes had had time to think, and so they were now quite optimistic about their chances of escaping.

It was just a question of agreeing on a plan.

'OK,' said Camicazi breezily. 'I've thought of several ways to escape. I might dress up as a Hysteric and trick one of those idiot guards into launching one of those little landing-boats by saying we'd hit an iceberg.'

'That Hysteric guard isn't going to think you're another Hysteric!' scoffed Fishlegs. 'However stupid they are they're not actually *blind*! You're only four foot tall, Camicazi, you're blonde, you're female, you have no facial hair...'

'*Aha*,' said Camicazi, laying a finger against her nose and looking very cunning, 'but if I wear a very long coat, and stand on your shoulders, and I'll stick one of Norbert's bearskin knee-pads on to my chin as a beard—'

'There's no way *in a million years* that that is going to work,' argued Fishlegs.

'OK, so what's YOUR idea, then, Mr Clever Clogs?' said Camicazi crossly. 'I'm telling you, I've escaped from more Uglithug Dungeons and Murderous Cage-Mazes than you've had hot dinners…'

Meanwhile, in the background, Norbert was watching the crew feeding the Wanderer Slaves by opening up the Slave Hatch and throwing food down below.

'Not TOO much of that bread,' Norbert roared greedily. 'They're refusing to row, and slaves that are on strike should not be fed.'

Unbeknownst to Norbert, Toothless was showing off his excellent hunting skills to Stormfly.

He had been chasing a fly through the rigging for the past five minutes. He was now hovering about a metre above Norbert's head, only his wings and his narrowed eyes moving as he watched the fly.

'Bzzz… bzzzzz… bzzzzzz…' buzzed the fly, zig-zagging drunkenly around Norbert's head.

Toothless crept ever so softly down in the air as his muscles poised, ready to pounce.

The fly made a few more aimless buzzes…

... and settled on the end of one of Norbert's sticking-up hairs.

'W-W-Wrrrewwwowwwwwrrrrrrrrrr!!!!!!!'

With the smothered yowl of a kung-fu kitten, Toothless launched himself, claws out, on to Norbert's head.

Norbert was not a relaxed personality. In fact, you *could* describe him as 'tightly wound'. So his reaction when a dragon suddenly landed unexpectedly on his head was to shriek like a fire-engine and spring into the air, as if stung by a bee. One of his flailing arms pushed over one of the Hysteric crew-members... who then cannoned into Hiccup... and Hiccup slid over, plunging down into the Hatch, *just* managing to grab hold of the edge of the Hatch as he fell, so he was still hanging on by one hand...

... until with a cry of 'Hiccup!' and Toothless still attached to his head, Norbert blundered forward

to try and help, and in the process trod heavily on
Hiccup's clinging fingers.

So that Hiccup let go and fell down the Hatch…

… the Hatch that Bearcub's Grandmother only
the day before had been warning that no Viking should
fall down OR ELSE…

… down that very same Hatch Hiccup fell, the
door clanging shut behind him.

There was a short silence.
Then pandemonium broke out.

'Aaaarrgh!' screeched Norbert the Nutjob, seeing his guide to America lost, and his journey going up in smoke. 'Get him out! Get him out! They'll kill him!'

But the crew could not open the Hatch. Somebody had lost the key and had to run off and find it.

Frantically, Camicazi and Fishlegs and Norbert pulled and pulled at the bars, and tried to squint down to see what was happening.

There was a horrible noise of shouting and screaming going on down there in the darkness.

What was happening to Hiccup?

Hiccup fell down, down, down, into the blackness of the hold, landing on the wood with the carrots, and the bread, and the cabbages the Wanderers were starting to eat.

There was a shocked silence for a moment.

Then came a roar of rage.

'**It's a Viking!**' yelled one big Wanderer, shaking his chains in fury.

'**Kill him!**' shrieked Bearcub's Grandmother, showing her sharp pointy teeth and seizing Hiccup by the leg. '**Crush him to death!**' She made a growling noise like a wolf.

'**It's quite a *small* Viking**,' said the big Wanderer more uncertainly as he grabbed hold of Hiccup, and he paused his raised hand.

Hiccup knew that all Wandering Peoples
could speak Dragonese as well as they
spoke their mother tongue.*

So he spoke to them directly
in the Dragonese language.

'Please don't kill me...'
whispered Hiccup.

There was
a moment's
astonished
silence.

Vikings are
VERMIN!

---

*Unlike Vikings, who had mostly lost the art of speaking
with serpents.

'It's a Viking that speaks Dragonese,' said Bearcub's Grandmother in amazement.

'Please don't kill me,' repeated Hiccup.

'Why should we not kill you?' asked Bearcub's Grandmother in a dreadful angry voice, her eyes as wide and staring and hypnotic as those of a king cobra.

'Your people have killed *my* people for as long as my people can remember. They have robbed us, and cheated us, and sold us into slavery. All of history is against you, Viking. Why should we not kill you?'

Hiccup had never met a Wanderer before, and she was an awful sight, her hair all askew like a bundle of hay, and those terrible grim and gloomy eyes, always staring into the far distance as if she'd just spotted something terrifying.

She took Hiccup by the neck in one of her skinny hands. 'You are a Viking, and all Vikings are vermin, wicked and brutish enslavers of dragons and humans. You may be young, but you should be killed *now* before you grow into a rat, or a fox,' she said, her voice shaking with fury. Her long fingernails dug scratches into Hiccup and he was petrified she was going to strangle him.

'We're not ALL like that,' protested Hiccup.

When Hiccup fell down the Hatch his helmet

had fallen off, and it was lying on the wooden floor beside him. Little Bearcub had been staring fixedly at Hiccup's bared head, and now he piped up, pointing at Hiccup's hair.

'Look, Grandmother, he hasn't got any horns.'

'What do you mean?' snapped Bearcub's grandmother.

'You said that Vikings were devils that had horns growing on their heads, which was why their helmets were such a funny shape,' said Bearcub. 'But look, this one doesn't.'

'Humph,' snorted Bearcub's grandmother, feeling through Hiccup's shaggy red hair. 'Perhaps they are too small to see yet. But, trust me, they are there. There's a few lumps and bumps here that could easily grow into horns.'

'If you don't kill me,' pleaded Hiccup desperately, 'I will help you.'

Bearcub's Grandmother gave a bitter laugh and shook her chains. 'Nobody can help us,' she said in Dragonese, opening up her gloomy eyes. 'We are DOOMED... we are ALL Doomed, for I have put a Curse upon this ship.'

'Yes, I heard,' said Hiccup nervously, thinking, *not another fruitcake*. 'But we are travelling north, where your people come from, and when we get closer to your country, I will help you to escape.'

There was a moment's silence, and then the listening Wanderers broke out in a chatter of excitement.

Bearcub's Grandmother was more sceptical. 'How can you do that?' she spat in disbelief. 'You are far too small...'

'I will find a way,' said Hiccup. 'I'm pretty sure I will, anyway. I've done this sort of thing before.'

There was a long, long silence. Everyone looked at Bearcub's Grandmother. She was staring at Hiccup, boring into him with her eyes, as if a tiny hope was struggling with a lifetime's bitter experience.

'You are a Viking,' she said at last. 'I think that you are saying this so that we will let you go, and you will climb back to freedom, and then forget about us.' She jerked her head up at the Hatch above, which the Vikings were still banging and clanging in their desperate attempts to open it.

'I give you my promise,' said Hiccup.

'A Viking's promise is worth nothing,' spat Bearcub's Grandmother. She looked at him thoughtfully. 'What is your name, Viking?' she asked.

'Hiccup Horrendous Haddock the Third,' replied

Hiccup. 'I am the son of Chief Stoick the Vast, of the Hooligan Tribe.'

'Viking *royalty*,' said Bearcub's Grandmother, sarcastically, but Hiccup had made her pause, and she was thinking hard. 'How interesting. We are honoured indeed. *King* Rat. *King* Fox.'

Her eye caught a long, sinister-looking metal tool leaning against one of the beams that propped up the ceiling of the hold. It ended in the shape of an 'S', and it was dipped in a dark blue ink.

the
slavemark

'OK then, Viking,' said Bearcub's Grandmother, 'you have got yourself a deal. But it will come at a price. In return I will give you the Slavemark. Hold him fast, Wildthing and Lonefox...'

'No!' screamed Hiccup, struggling frantically.

'The Slavemark is easy to give,' said Bearcub's Grandmother slowly, approaching him with the pointed stick, 'but impossible to remove.' She pointed bitterly at the blue Mark on her hand.

119

'Take off his helmet,' Bearcub's Grandmother ordered Wildthing and Lonefox. 'And then he can hide it from those devil-Vikings up there. We do not want them to suspect that he has an understanding with us.'

So Bearcub's Grandmother put the Mark on the side of Hiccup's head, some way above his left ear. One second later and the Slavemark was there, a livid blue mark that would stay for ever, a bit like a tattoo.

'You will not be able to forget us now,' said Bearcub's Grandmother with gloomy satisfaction.

The Hatch above Hiccup's head finally burst open and a great shaft of light poured into the dark room.

Norbert the Nutjob's furious red screaming face appeared in the space. 'IF YOU'VE TOUCHED A HAIR ON HIS HEAD I'LL FEED THE LOT OF YOU TO THE LOBSTERS!' he roared. 'CLIMB UP *QUICK* THERE, BOY!'

A rope flopped down into the hold.

'Swear by this Mark that you will help us escape, or we will not let you go,' hissed Bearcub's Grandmother.

'I swear,' gasped Hiccup, nearly crying. And then he put both hands upon the rope, and was hauled up through the Hatch.

'You see, Grandmother!' said Bearcub excitedly, 'We are not Doomed after all! I asked for someone to rescue us and he *has!*'

'You are not rescued *yet*,' said his Grandmother sternly.

The Hatch clanged shut and they were left in darkness again.

'And wipe your nose,' came the voice of Bearcub's Grandmother in the blackness. 'It's running most dreadfully.'

We're saved!

9. THE LAND OF THE POLAR-SERPENTS

The *American Dream II* puffed its way steadily north, and the weather got colder and colder, and darker and darker, until they were travelling through total blackness, day and night, and this was the home of the Wanderers.

It was an eerie place. Icebergs drifted by, taller than the masts of the ship itself, cracking and splitting and creaking around them in the mist.

The crew fell silent as they went about their work, and even Norbert managed to lower his voice to a menacing whisper as he scolded and shook his axe threateningly at his men.

For they had entered the world of the Polar-serpents.

The Polar-serpents were great white dragons slumbering on the ice like over-sized walruses. They reminded Hiccup of the Sabre-tooth Driver Dragons the Vikings used to pull their sleds back in the Archipelago. Except that instead of sabre-teeth, out of the nose of each Polar-serpent grew a long white tusk like a unicorn or a narwhal.

Polar-serpents swam under the icebergs, and when they found shoals of unwary seals and penguins resting on the surface above, they sawed great holes in the ice, so that the unsuspecting prey fell into their open jaws below.

A Polar-serpent feeding frenzy was a terrifying sight. They could strip a mammal down to the bone far quicker than a shoal of piranhas, and as far as they were concerned, a human was just as tasty as a seal.

Perhaps even tastier.

Of course, the Polar-serpents weren't a threat when you were aboard a boat... but nonetheless,

polar-serpents

~STATISTICS~

COLOURS: White with faint grey markings
ARMED WITH: Talons and spear-like horn
FEAR FACTOR:..............6
ATTACK:.........................7
SPEED:................................7
SIZE:.......................................5
DISOBEDIENCE:................6

Polar-serpents live in the north, basking like
seals on flat icebergs. Their beauty hides a
cruel streak. A pack will even attack a polar
bear. They nest in snowdrifts, crevasses
and on the tops of icebergs. They windsurf
across the ice on their tummies and reach
extraordinary speeds doing this.

Hiccup swallowed hard as they steamed quietly past the creatures. And he noticed that all of Norbert's hunting-dragons were careful to stay close to the ship as well.

They roosted on the masts like a row of malevolent starlings, watching the Polar-serpents, with the Polar-serpents watching them back.

After a while Norbert slightly lost it with the Polar-serpents.

'STOP LOOKING AT ME, YOU BIG WHITE MAGGOTS!' he yelled, waving his axe at the dragons. 'OR I'LL CLIMB OVERBOARD AND CHOP OFF YOUR HORNS!'

He grabbed the cauldron with the remains of lunch and shook it over the side of the boat.

The statues on the ice sprang instantly to life. They slid into the water like big white crocodiles: thirty, forty, fifty, sixty, three hundred of them.

Within about five seconds the water behind the boat was a thrashing, churning, manic froth of red as the Polar-serpents went into their feeding frenzy.

They were so crazy in their bloodlust that they even attacked each other, tearing each other from limb to limb.

Norbert went back to whispering.

The Slavemark
is easy to give
but impossible
to remove.

All day long, Hiccup could feel the Slavemark pressing against his helmet. He hadn't told Fishlegs and Camicazi about it, because he knew he had to keep it a secret. The Law of the Archipelago was quite firm upon the matter. Anybody with the Slavemark was automatically an Outcast, whether it was their fault or not.

And they certainly couldn't become a *Chief*. No, if Hiccup ever got back home (and it was a big 'if' at this point), this was a secret that Hiccup would have to keep to himself for the rest of his life. He couldn't tell anybody, because if someone like Snotlout were to find out...

Hiccup pushed the thought to the back of his mind, because he had to concentrate on the more pressing problem of escaping.

And now, escaping had been made that much more difficult. As Camicazi had so helpfully pointed out, it was all very well trying to escape when there are three of you, but trying to get a hundred and twenty-two people off a ship without their captors noticing required a little more forward planning.

'We could escape so easily on our *own*,' complained Camicazi. 'Why are you suddenly bothering about those people? They're not even Vikings, they're WANDERERS, for Thor's sake, we might set them free and then they might kill us, you know what people say about Wanderers.'

'I told you,' said Hiccup grumpily. 'I had to make them a promise.'

Hiccup sat up in the crow's nest of the *American Dream II*, and thought and thought and thought, his legs swinging as Stormfly and Toothless chased each other round and round in circles.

In the middle of the night...

I am very hungry

Me has b-b-buckets di belly-scream.
I am very hungry.

Me isna burped si ISSA middling
o di zuzztime.
*I don't care if it IS the middle
of the night.*

Me needy di grubbings SNIP-SNAP!
I want food RIGHT NOW!

Oo mes'll do di
yowlyshreekers too
fortissimo theys'll earwig me
indi BigManGaff.
Or I'll scream so loudly they'll hear me in Valhalla.

Or I'll scream so
loudly they'll hear
me in Valhalla

Me needy di S-S-S-S-SALTSICKS.
I want OYSTERS.

Yow g-g-grabba di saltsicks low indi Landscoop. Sna
staraway.
*You can get oysters from the Harbour.
It's not far.*

M-M-Me gogo ta yowlshreek...
I'm starting to scream...
(three quarters of an hour later)

Yow me p-p-peepers undo!
You woke me up!

Wah is DA?
What is THAT?

Da na goggle com s-s-
saltsicks...
That doesn't look like oysters...

DA goggle com sniffersludge...
THAT looks like bogeys...

THAT looks like bogeys

Sniffersludge p-p-plus di squidink tiddles...
Bogeys with black bits in them...

Me no likeit di squidink tiddles.
Issa y-y-yuck-yuck.
I don't like black bits. They're disgusting.

They're
disgustery

Watever, me is tow zuzzready
por di scrumming.
*Anyway, I'm too
tired to eat.*

Why are you
in a bad mood?

10. TOOTHLESS'S ADVENTURE IN THE COOKING TENT

It was Toothless who provided the answer to the Escape Problem.

One afternoon Hiccup looked down from the crow's nest and spotted Stormfly and Toothless creeping out of the Cooking Tent. They had sneaked in there while the Cook was having a thoughtful chat with Norbert, as Norbert checked his Great Map of America.

Both dragons were flying extremely erratically. Stormfly had turned every colour of the rainbow, and was letting out little hiccups in fiery explosions of golden smoke as she somersaulted and cartwheeled through the air.

Toothless appeared to be flying upside-down.

He too was hiccupping, and with every hiccup, a little stream of golden bubbles blew out of his nose.

'What ARE they doing?' asked Camicazi, in danger of falling off the mast as she peered down at the little dragons' eccentric progress.

'They look like they're DRUNK,' said Fishlegs in amazement.

Toothless got entangled in the rigging, and the

Stormfly was so helpless with giggles she could barely free him.

'Isshh v-v-very TANGLY, thish air,' Hiccup could hear Toothless saying.

Eventually they got going again, and they flew past Hiccup's perch.

'Who ISH this tall gentleman?' asked Toothless, as he bashed into the mast for the second time. 'He keepsh getting in my way.'

'Toothless! Stormfly!' Hiccup called out. 'Come over here!'

'That b-b-boy over there s-s-seemsh to be calling you,' Toothless advised the Stormfly. 'Hic... whoops... shorry...'

They flapped over to where Hiccup and Camicazi and Fishlegs were sitting, and they were burping and swaying and exploding with bubbles.

'What *have* you been doing?' scolded Hiccup. 'I TOLD you not to go near that Cooking Tent...'

'I haven't been anywhere near the Cooking Tent, have you, Toothless?' drawled Stormfly.

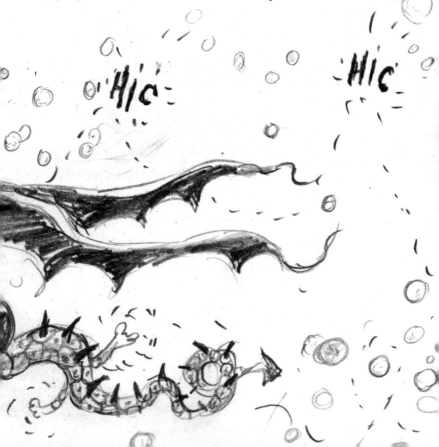

The upside-down Toothless nodded so hard great streams of golden bubbles poured out of his ears.

'Abshotutely NOT,' he said solemnly, his eyes crossing. 'T-t-toothless NOT go into the Cooking Tent... Toothless N-N-NOT open the lovely shcrum-diddly-delicious j-j-jar of lemonade with the l-l-lovely tickly bubbles... oooh... hic... tee hee... there goes another one... Toothless not there... Toothless... Toothless...'

He searched his rather addled brain for a really good excuse this time, and came up with a **BELTER**. 'Toothless in *R-R-Rome*,' he said at last.

'Really?' said Hiccup politely, carefully turning Toothless the right way up, and settling him in his arms.

'OR up the chimney,' said Toothless, not quite able to decide which was more convincing. 'With Toothless's *good friend*, the s-s-senator.'

And with that, both Toothless and the Stormfly fell asleep, so suddenly and deeply that the Stormfly fell off her perch, and Camicazi only just caught her in time.

They were both snoring like two little hibernating grizzly bears.

All around their mouths was a slightly sticky browny-yellow substance.

'*Dragon-nip*,' said Hiccup thoughtfully. 'There must be a jar of dragon-nip down there in the Cooking Tent.'

Dragon-nip was a perfectly harmless but sleep-inducing substance gathered from the sweat glands of the Loafer dragon.

'A spot of dragon-nip in the dinner, and anybody who eats it will be out for the count for the next twelve hours…' said Hiccup. 'OK, guys. I think this could be a good night for us to escape.'

11. THE ESCAPE FROM THE AMERICAN DREAM II

The full moon shone down on the great boat steaming through the icebergs. The crew of the *American Dream II* feasted well that night, on a stew which, unbeknownst to them, was heavily laced with dragon-nip.

Hiccup had crept in to the Cooking Tent, and poured it into the bubbling cauldron of dinner.

For a while the Hysterical crew ignored their spooky surroundings, and sang out loud songs to the moon above, banging their dinner plates on the deck, and Norbert the Nutjob fiddled madly on his Viking violin, and the Hysterics did wild jigs, and the Polar-serpents sat on their icebergs, quiet statues, only their eyes following the mayhem.

And then, one by one, the dragon-nip's heavy fumes overcame the Hysterics. Sleep overtook them so quickly that they dropped as they stood, in the middle of whatever they happened to be doing at the time, and fell to the deck in grotesque attitudes of slumber.

Norbert lay snoring, the violin still tucked under his chin. Goggle-eyes the Gory was clasped fondly to the breast of Verociously Violent, who was under the sleepy delusion that he was three years old again, and this was his mother.

Red Ronald was pedalling the wheels of the Keep-the-Boat-from-Sinking-and-Scare-Away-the-Big-Sea-Creatures Machine slower and slower until he stopped entirely and drooped snoring over the handlebars.

And the Ship's Cook collapsed face down in his snail and jellyfish pie. (He would still be picking bits of snail shell and egg out of his nostrils three days later.)

Hiccup, Camicazi and Fishlegs waited till everybody on the deck was completely still – and then they waited five minutes more, just to make sure. Then slowly, quietly, they slipped down the rigging of the mast. Hiccup was carrying the sleeping Toothless in his breast pocket, and Camicazi had the slumbering Stormfly draped around her shoulders like a scarf.

They tip-toed across the deck of the *American Dream II*, carefully, *carefully* picking their way through the sleeping, snoring Warriors lying strewn on the boards, the sweet yellow-brown smoke from the cauldron billowing across the ship and making their eyes water. Cautiously, gently, Hiccup took the ticking-thing from around Norbert's wrist, and tied it back again to his own.

Quietly, softly, Camicazi removed the large bunch of keys from Norbert's waistband with her quick, light little fingers, and she opened the lock of the Hatch that led down to the hold where they were holding the Wanderers. It took all three of them to lift up the Hatch, which they did with a whining C-C-C-CREAK! And then they threw down a rope and the keys to the Wanderers below, Hiccup whispering as loud as he dared to tell them to unlock their chains and climb up, one by one.

The first two out were Bearcub and his Grandmother.

Bearcub was in a state of high excitement, and danced round his Grandmother squeaking, 'I TOLD you! I TOLD you he would rescue us! You see! You see! Not ALL Vikings are wicked, and we're not DOOMED after all!'

Bearcub's Grandmother was torn between her delight at being rescued, and her annoyance that her prophecy of DOOM wasn't being fulfilled. 'Mff,' she sniffed. 'We're not rescued YET. If just one of those Vikings wakes up, we're all as dead as dinosaurs... DOOMED, the lot of us... a one-way ticket to the happy hunting grounds...'

'Can you work out how to get back to your home

from here?' asked Hiccup, consulting the ticking-thing anxiously. 'And take us back to Berk when you've got there?'

The scary white wilderness all around them seemed an unlikely sort of home to Hiccup, but there was a happy glint in Bearcub's Grandmother's wild eyes, although she tried to hide it. She breathed in the air, as cold as needles, and peered through the mists as if looking at something very familiar. She nodded. 'A Wanderer is never lost,' she said. 'We don't need that silly little bauble of yours to take us home. I could have showed that ridiculous Viking with the axe the way to America, if he'd had the intelligence to ask me...'

Hiccup tried to organise launching the landing-boats in a QUIET sort of way, which was impossible, and Hiccup hopped from foot to foot in anxiety as the Hysterical Warriors mumbled in their sleep with every crash of the oars. They were heavily armed, with swords, and wicked axes, and every sort of dagger, and Bearcub's Grandmother did have a point: Hiccup had no doubt that if awoken, they would deal out death with a vengeance.

But it seemed that luck was with the escapers.

The seven landing-boats plopped into the water without any of the Hysterics opening their eyes.

The Wanderers filled the boats, and the first boat began to row through the mists, Bearcub's Grandmother standing up straight and tall at the front, pointing the way with one outstretched arm.

The last landing-boat had filled up, apart from Hiccup, Fishlegs and Camicazi.

Fishlegs was watching Hiccup, as Hiccup got ready to climb down over the rim of the *American Dream II* and into the last landing-boat.

There were flat icebergs very close to the left and right of them. Camicazi had taken over from the snoring Red Ronald, and was steering the *American Dream II*, making sure the ship was moving forward in a straight line so that it didn't bump into the icebergs. She had tied the slumbering Stormfly to her chest, and the little dragon suddenly stirred violently in her sleep, jogging Camicazi's arm on the steering wheel... the *American Dream II* swerved suddenly and violently to the left...

... *just* as Hiccup was dangling over the edge on a rope, preparing to let himself drop into the little boat filled with Wanderers below.

'Wooooahhhhh!' gasped Hiccup, as the rope swung him forward, leaving the landing-boat behind. 'Watch where you're going, Camicazi!'

142

But Stormfly seemed to be
having some sort of nightmare, and
was squirming around wildly, so that
Camicazi was struggling to see over
her wriggling tail as it flapped in
Camicazi's face. In those vital
seconds, the *American
Dream II*
careered
erratically
forward,
glancing off an
iceberg to the left,
before Stormfly

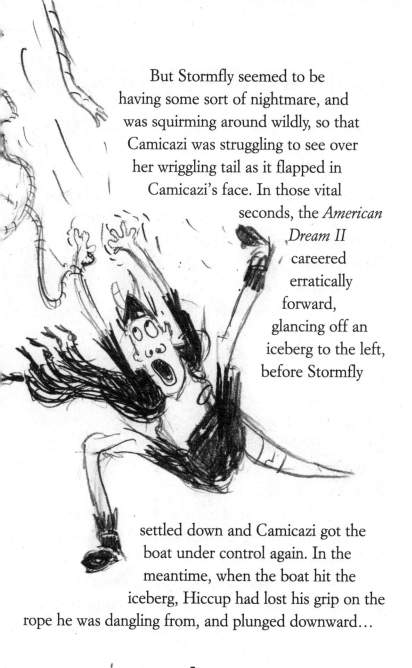

settled down and Camicazi got the
boat under control again. In the
meantime, when the boat hit the
iceberg, Hiccup had lost his grip on the
rope he was dangling from, and plunged downward…

12. R-R-R-R-UUUUNNNNNNN!!!!!

… and landed, rather painfully, on his bottom, RIGHT in the middle of a circle of Polar-serpents.

Slowly the Polar-serpents' heads turned one hundred and eighty degrees, like the heads of owls, to look at Hiccup.

'OK...' stammered Hiccup. 'Easy now... nice Polar-serpents... *sweet* Polar-serpents... what lovely sharp horns you have...'

'All the better,' whined the nearest Polar-serpent, 'for spearing you with.'

ck tock

tick tock

'R-R-R-R-R-U-U-U-U-U-U-U-UNNNNNN!!!!!' shouted Camicazi from the deck of the *American Dream II*.

Hiccup didn't need to be told.

He scrambled to his feet, slipping and sliding on the slippery ice.

The Polar-serpent has a very strange way of manouvering across the ice floes, and if Hiccup hadn't been right in the middle of fleeing for his life, he

144

might have admired it. Half the pack of Polar-serpents spread out their wings like the sails of ships, braced their talons, and then shot forward on their smooth bellies, rocketing after Hiccup, their noses pointed straight toward him like darts for a dartboard. The remaining Polar-serpents slid into the water, swift and silent as alligators, and joined the chase from under the ice.

'Don't fall over, don't fall over, don't fall over!' begged Hiccup, clasping Toothless to his chest to stop him falling out of his waistcoat as he ran. He could hear the Polar-serpents whirring closer and closer, their nails screeching on the ice.

Now the shadows of those that were swimming under the ice swooped like swallows under his feet.

The *American Dream II* was still steaming alongside the iceberg.

'Hang on, Hiccup!' shouted Camicazi at the steering wheel. 'We're coming to rescue you!'

But Hiccup had no intention of hanging on. He was running faster than he ever had done in his life.

'**Mfff**,' sniffed Bearcub's Grandmother. '**It doesn't look good**.' She tut-tutted. '**He's not long for this world, you mark my words**.'

She held up a skinny finger. '**He's DOOMED, I tell you, DOOMED**.'

It seemed a fairly safe prediction, under the circumstances.

CCCC-CCC—RRUNNNNNK!

A great horn speared up through the ice right in front of Hiccup.

He swerved around it in the nick of time.

CCCC-CCCCRUNNNNK! CRRRUNNK! CRUNNNNKK!!!!

Three more appeared, and Hiccup slalomed round *them* too.

'*Kill them!*' shrieked Camicazi.

Fishlegs had got hold of one of Norbert's great bow-and-arrow harpoons.

tick-tock

It is unclear how he thought he was going to kill FIFTY Polar-serpents with the one harpoon, but he was pointing it in the general direction of the Polar-serpents with the bow upside-down, and his eyes shut.

As the harpoon went off Fishlegs fell backwards, letting go of the bow, which ricocheted across the deck, and jammed itself under the rim of the boat.

The harpoon sailed through the air, missing the Polar-serpents by at least ten metres.

But it was right bang on target for Hiccup, and would have hit him splang in the chest if the rope hadn't run out and pulled it to a sharp halt, sending it crashing to the ice with a clang.

'Why are you shooting at *me*?' howled a sprinting Hiccup. 'Haven't I got enough problems?'

The harpoon clattered in front of him, setting off little sprays of snow as it bounced across the ice.

'Oh *I* see…' panted Hiccup, and he launched himself at the harpoon as it dragged off…

But he *just* missed catching hold of the rope with both hands.

'Great God Thor… *ow!*… I could do… with some HELP here…' begged Hiccup, his chin in the snow.

But it seemed the Great God Thor was

148

temporarily deaf. The Polar-serpents were closing in for the kill, sending out thunderbolts of flame that only just missed incinerating poor Hiccup.

Hiccup scrambled to his feet. The harpoon was way out of reach now, his last hope of getting back on board the boat. The iceberg stretched out flat in front of him. He knew he couldn't outrun the Polar-serpents, who were already gaining on him. To his left there was a gigantic cliff of ice, with an enormous dark Cave at the bottom of it, like the open mouth of a monster.

Hiccup ran full tilt into the Cave.

The Polar-serpents followed.

He could hear their talons clicking and scraping on the ice, and their quick, fast breathing, so close that they were trying to grab hold of the ticking-thing bouncing along behind him, like great cats pouncing on a tasty morsel tied to the end of a string.

What's that up ahead? thought Hiccup. *Oh Woden the Great and Magnificent, I am begging you, please don't let that be a wall, the finish of the Cave, a dead-end, in which case I really* am *dead...*

It *was* a wall.

But as Hiccup ran closer still, he could see it was a rough and craggy wall with nooks and crannies and

ledges and knobbly bits, and if he could climb up it
before the Polar-serpents caught him, surely there
would be a tunnel up there somewhere…

*O Bending Biceps and Quivering Quadrapeds
and Twitching Toenails and Little Hairy Curly Bits of
Thunderous Thor!!!!!*

It wasn't a wall at all. It was a DRAGON.

He was running straight, full-tilt, as hard as he
could towards a truly immense sleeping Sea-dragon, so
huge that its head filled the entire cave in front of him.

Hiccup put the brakes on.

He skidded abruptly, screeching on the ice, slid
forward, arms waggling desperately, trying to stop

before he bumped into the thing, because he really
did NOT want to wake it up…

… and he came to a halt just in the *nick* of time,
feet away from the dragon's sleeping chin.

Hiccup stopped.

But the ticking-thing attached to Hiccup's wrist
did not stop.

Momentum carried the ticking-thing UP from
the ice where it had been bouncing along behind

Hiccup, sailing o-o-o-over Hiccup's head, and on and on and up… and landing, sharp and precise, on the closed eyelid of the sleeping dragon, as if it were politely, but firmly, knocking on a door.

'Oh brother… oh brother… oh brother…' whispered Hiccup, reeling the ticking-thing in and around his wrist.

The eyelid fluttered.

It stayed down, as Hiccup backed slowly away.

'Please stay closed… please stay closed… please stay closed…'

And then the eye opened.

In the darkness of the Cave it was like turning on a great yellow searchlight, and Hiccup was blinded by the glare.

How quickly the hunters become the hunted.

Hiccup was now running TOWARDS the Polar-serpents, confusing them considerably... until they too realised that that bright light was in fact the eye of an enormous, no-longer-sleeping, dragon.

Yowling and screeching like a pack of wolves, the Polar-serpents came tumbling and somersaulting to a stop and turned to run back the other way, with Hiccup belting after them, arms and legs going like pistons.

And behind them the terrible beginnings of a great rumbling R-R-R-ROAR...

The *American Dream II* had passed on from the iceberg now,

and was some distance away, and Camicazi was trying to get it to turn around.

Fishlegs looked over his shoulder to see the entire pack of Polar-serpents shooting out of the great Ice Cave like arrows shot from a bow.

Followed by Hiccup, running flat out.

'What's… going… on?' asked Fishlegs, knowing that whatever it was, it was Very Bad News.

The flat iceberg stretched out in front of Hiccup, far too big for safety. There was nowhere to go, no trees to hide under. No rocks, no tunnels for shelter.

So there wasn't really any point in running.

But the young Viking and the Polar-serpents still ran, nonetheless, hoping to put off their deaths for one moment, one *second* even.

For to Fishlegs's horror, two great yellow eyes slowly appeared in the darkness of the mouth of the Ice Cave.

Whatever it was, it was *huge*.

Something
like a moving
mountain with
wings exploded
out of the Cave.
The cliff erupted
into a volcano of
snow, as this *Something* burst out
of there. A great mass of raw
energy, a roar of wild triumph
screaming from its throat,
sending snow and ice
exploding in all
directions.

It was so big it momentarily blotted out the moon as it sailed through the air, and landed, screaming, on the iceberg Hiccup was running across.

So big was this Thing, that when the Thing landed, it crashed through the entire iceberg, sending great slabs of ice, and fountains of water, shooting up into the air. And Hiccup and the Polar-serpents were catapulted upwards.

The Polar-serpents ricocheted off in all directions like fireworks.

And up and up Hiccup sailed… o-o-o-o-o-over the surprised, sinking Monster's head… across the sea… up and towards the deck of the *American Dream II*… where he *just* missed catching on to the rim of the boat with his flailing fingers, and fell down, down, the side of the boat, and into the sea.

Where he would have remained if the harpoon that Fishlegs had shot earlier hadn't snagged into the back of his waistcoat, and dragged him along as if the boat had caught itself a fish.

Hand over hand, Hiccup heaved himself up the rope, and Camicazi and Fishlegs hauled him up and on to the deck of the *American Dream II*, steaming westward with its still-sleeping crew. And as he clambered, dripping, over the edge of the boat, heart racing like a rabbit, scarcely able to believe that he was still alive...

'The Machine!' he gasped, and immediately ran to the Stop-the-Boat-From-Sinking-and-Scare-Away-the-Monster-Sea-Creatures Machine. 'Help me get this guy off it, Fishlegs.'

The two young Vikings dragged the dead-to-the-world Red Ronald off the Machine, and Hiccup looked fearfully over his shoulder. The Monster had disappeared underneath the broken remains of the iceberg it had shattered. But was it his imagination, or could he see a racing, shooting, white line of water, beginning to TURN AROUND, and move back in their direction...?

Hiccup thrust his trembling feet into the pedals of the Machine and circled them furiously, making the ridiculous trumpet-like thingy revolve like a whirligig.

'I thought you said that Machine was useless,' panted Fishlegs.

'Well, hopefully I was wrong,' gasped Hiccup. 'Because otherwise we are DEAD.'

'Full steam ahead!' shouted Camicazi, rushing back to the steering wheel of the boat, and the *American Dream II* surged away from the iceberg.

'I... think... it's... working...' panted Hiccup.

Thor only knew *how* the Machine worked,* but that white wake of water seemed to slow down... and slow down... and slow down... and finally turn away. So whether or not Norbert's Machine would prevent a boat from sinking, it did seem that it was not quite as loopy as it looked, and it really *could* scare away a Monster Sea-dragon.

With a massive sigh of relief, Hiccup turned and he looked back over his other shoulder... to see the seven boats of Wanderers oaring away from them as quickly as possible in the other direction.

'Hey!' cried Hiccup in alarm. He showered Fishlegs with drops of seawater as he waved his arms at them. 'Fishlegs, take over, and for Thor's sake **DON'T STOP PEDALLING...**'

Hiccup swapped places with Fishlegs, and ran up and down the deck shouting: 'Don't leave us! What are you doing? Come and get us! What are they doing?

---

* In his later memoirs, Hiccup suggests that the 'trumpet' attachment emitted an unbearable noise at a pitch too high for the human ear to hear. Other sources say that the hearing of the larger Sea-dragons was so acute they could pick up the noise of a shrimp breathing several miles away, and this would certainly explain why the Machine worked on the 'Dragon-Mammoths', but not on smaller dragons such as Polar-serpents.

Camicazi, turn round and go after them.'

'Are you CRAZY?' interrupted Fishlegs. 'What about that THING? We have to get out of here as quickly as possible.'

'WHERE ARE YOU GOING?' Hiccup cupped his hands and shouted through the swiftly descending sea mist at the Wanderers, fast disappearing in the other direction. Hiccup's heart sank. He couldn't believe the injustice of it. After ALL that he had done, ALL that they had risked to save them from slavery, the Wanderers were running away, abandoning them!

'COWARDS!' yelled Camicazi over her shoulder. 'YELLOWBELLIES! TRAITORS!'

For a few minutes, Hiccup could still see
Bearcub's Grandmother, standing straight and tall on
the edge of her boat.

And then she disappeared into the mist.

Z..Z..Z..Z

13. THEY WERE IN *ITS* TERRITORY NOW...

So that was the end of the last hope of Escape from the Quest to America.

All hundred and nineteen of the Wanderer Slaves escaped.

But Hiccup, Camicazi and Fishlegs did not.

Hiccup saved Bearcub.

But who would save Hiccup?

They had their work cut out over the next five hours or so, trying to prevent the great boat from crashing into an iceberg in the mist. And by the time the mists lifted it was nearly morning, they had steamed out of the land of the Icebergs and into the Great West Ocean, and the Hysterics were beginning to stir in their sleep.

It was astonishing that they had all slept through the whole thing, but they had, even Toothless, who had snored happily through being chased by Polar-serpents and bumping over icebergs and submerged in ice-cold water, without so much as opening an eyelid.

Red Ronald was the first to wake up, to find Camicazi pedalling the Keep-the-Boat-from-Sinking-and-Scare-Away-the-Monster-Sea-Creatures Machine.

'*I* won't tell Norbert, if you don't,' said Camicazi, climbing off the Machine and letting Red Ronald climb back on again. Red Ronald was so pathetically grateful he practically cried, for he knew if his Boss found out he had fallen asleep on the job he would quickly find himself on the wrong side of the Axe of Doom.

Hiccup re-tied the ticking-thing to Norbert's wrist, so that Norbert would never know he had tried to steal it, and then he judged it best that the three of them should be out of the way when Norbert made the discovery that all of his slaves had escaped into the night.

So, once Hiccup's clothes had thoroughly dried on the chimney, they crept back up to the crow's nest, where they fell asleep, curled around the comforting warmth of the two dragons, who gave out lovely waves of heat like two little hot water bottles. They were only awoken by Norbert's great roar of rage.

At first Norbert was sure that it was all Hiccup's fault.

'THAT WRETCHED WEIRD LITTLE RED-HAIRED BOY! I SHOULD HAVE KILLED HIM WHILE I HAD THE CHANCE!' screamed Norbert the Nutjob. 'HE'S MADE OFF WITH ALL OF MY SLAVES!'

Hiccup put his head over the top of the crow's nest.

'No, I haven't,' he called down. 'I'm up here...'

Norbert was so furious, he swiped at the mast with his Axe as if he were chopping down a tree, taking a big slice *out* of it. 'WHAT HAVE YOU DONE WITH MY SLAVES???!!!' he roared.

'I haven't done ANYTHING with your slaves,' Hiccup called down. 'If I *had* done, I would have run away myself.'

This was quite a good argument, but Norbert wasn't in a listening kind of mood and he took another swing at the mast.

'Now, now,' Hiccup shouted, 'we need that mast, you know, and I'm the only one who can read the ticking-thing and get us to America, aren't I? So without *me*, you can't create your Land of the Nutjobs... your Empire...'

With a massive effort, Norbert managed to stop himself from cutting down the mast. But nonetheless, Hiccup thought he might stay up in the crow's nest until he felt Norbert had calmed down.

Toothless and Stormfly both woke up much, much later, when the sun was high in the sky, and the two little dragons had absolutely no recollection of what had happened.

The ship was way out in the Great West Ocean now. The world around them had turned to water.

Nothing but water, water everywhere.

It was as if a Great Flood had taken place and washed over every precious piece of land. And now there was nothing but sea below and clouds above, and their tiny little speck of a boat crawling across it, like a bug across a window pane.

It was as if they had left this world entirely and were sailing through space, looking for another star. There was no way of contacting other humans. They were on their own, in a universe of water that went on for ever.

And what was worse, was that the ship now seemed to be being *followed* by something.

From high up in the crow's nest, Hiccup, Fishlegs and Camicazi saw it first.

It was the white wake of a GIGANTIC *Sea-Monster*.

'SEA-DRAGON ON THE EASTERN HORIZON!' screamed Norbert from down below on the deck. '*GET PEDALLING!!!!! OR I'LL FEED YOU TO THE MONSTER WITH MY OWN FAIR HANDS!!!*

The crew took it in turns to pedal the Scare-Away-the-Big-Sea-Creatures Machine so fast that the Machine's spokes and wheels whined a screeching, creaking, out-of-control complaint, and the trumpet-attachment thingy whirled so crazily, it looked in danger of falling off.

But the Sea-dragon was not scared away. The sound the Machine made was so physically unbearable to the Monster that it kept a safe distance from the boat. But it did not stop it from following them.

All of the rest of that day the Sea-dragon followed the *American Dream II*, and all of the night.

The crew went to sleep at their battle-stations, upright in their armour, harpoons at the ready.

As they closed their eyes in sleep, it was the last thing they saw on the horizon, the long thin line of a white wake, and the great spiny back of one of the Great, Deadly Terrors of the Deep, rising and falling as it swam inexorably after them like some ghastly Fate.

They were in ITS territory now...

... and IT knew it.

All it had to do, was to be patient.

The only thing preventing the Sea-dragon from moving in for the kill, and tearing apart the *American Dream II* with its mighty jaws as if it were a child's toy, was a dilapidated, cranky, over-worked little Machine.

A Machine that was looking increasingly creaky and wonky as each crew member pedalled it furiously to death.

If a screw came loose on one of those wobbling wheels, that whirligig trumpet thingy would come whizzing off and...

It didn't bear thinking about.

EVERYBODY had nightmares that night.

And it made Hiccup's heart skip a beat or two when he woke to see the wake of the Sea-dragon on the horizon. It was still following them.

Hiccup crept down from the crow's nest, and over to the Steering Deck where Norbert was staring at it too, through his looking-glass thingy.

'Norbert,' said Hiccup nervously. 'I just have a feeling that that Sea-dragon doesn't like us for some reason. Don't you think we should go home?'

For a moment, Hiccup didn't think Norbert had heard him, for Norbert carried on looking at the horizon, muttering to himself slowly: *'That...* is the largest Sea-Monster I have EVER seen...'

And then Norbert took his looking-glass thingy from his eye and looked straight down at Hiccup.

'No dragon, however big, is going to take away

my dream,' ground out Norbert the Nutjob from between clenched teeth, shaking his fist in Hiccup's face. 'I'll jump down that Thing's throat and personally remove its wishbone with my axe if I have to. You understand me, boy?'

Hiccup nodded.

'DEATH or AMERICA!' roared Norbert the Nutjob. 'Now read me the ticking-thing, and stop talking treachery.'

Hiccup climbed despondently back to the crow's nest, and relayed the bad news to his friends.

'This just gets worse and worse, it's like some sort of nightmare...' moaned Fishlegs. 'We could have escaped on our own, but, oh no, you have to choose to try and escape with a hundred and nineteen Wanderers, very subtle, and they aren't even Vikings...'

'I made them a promise,' replied Hiccup automatically.

'And look how they repaid you!!' Fishlegs pointed out. 'So you've saved a hundred and nineteen not-very-nice complete strangers, but you've doomed your two best friends in the process. Nice choice, Hiccup. Any escape plans, Camicazi?'

Even Camicazi, who had escaped from practically every Tribe in the Archipelago, seemed to have run out of hope that she could escape from this situation. 'I think the safest place to be right now is on this ship,' she said. 'Because out there, is that Sea-dragon. Do you think it's the same one that chased you in the land of the Polar-serpents?'

'Definitely,' said Hiccup. 'I recognised the spines on its back. Those kind of spikes are mostly seen on dragons that are now extinct.'

'What kind of dragon is it, anyway?' asked Fishlegs.

'I don't know,' said Hiccup slowly. 'It was difficult to tell because it was so dark, but it wasn't a species I recognised. It reminds me of some of the ones that I've heard about in the ancient Sagas. A Leviathorgan, or a Gorgenghast.'

'Aren't those just mythical creatures?' asked Camicazi. 'You know, made-up, like unicorns and mermaids and things?'

'Maybe they're *not* made-up,' said Hiccup. 'Maybe they just haven't been seen for a long time. Just because we don't know *how* that Machine works, doesn't mean that it *doesn't* work. Just because we've never *seen* America, doesn't mean it isn't *there*. We're in waters that we're not used to now, the waters of the Great West Ocean. There could be all *sorts* of terrible things down there in the fathoms below us, who knows?'

It was not a cheerful thought.

To keep their spirits up, they thought about what everybody would be doing back at home.

The Hooligan Tribe would be back on Berk now, playing Bashyball in the mud, preparing for the spring shearing, painting the boats for the summer sailings.

'I wonder who won the Inter-Tribe Friendly Swimming Race?' mused Fishlegs.

'My mother is the Archipelago Long Distance Swimming Champion, Bertha the Unsinkable!' said Camicazi. 'She'd have stayed out there for *days*!'

'And why wouldn't my father have won?' argued Hiccup loyally. 'He's just as good at swimming as Bertha...'

'NO WAY!' insisted Camicazi.

And so they argued, back and forth, not that it mattered, of course, but it passed the time, and it helped to be thinking of what might be happening at home.

They did not realise, of course, that in fact neither of their parents had actually *left the beach*, let alone *won the Competition*, on that fateful morning several weeks ago...

14. WHAT HAPPENED BACK IN THE MURDEROUS MOUNTAINS

Several weeks earlier, back in the Murderous Mountains, it looked like Madguts would have the glory of being Last Man Back. He lasted for forty-one hours out there in the water, which, even when covered with a thin layer of Deepest Purple Fleshfang Oil, is an almost superhuman feat.

He was greeted by a cheering crowd of Viking Tribesmen on the Long Beach as he strode out of the waves, arms held above his head in victory, Gumboil trotting a few steps in front of him.

The Chief Judge, the sad little Bashem-Oik, rushed up the beach to meet Madguts. He gave him a golden medal, and a pipe that Madguts jammed between his lips as he made a Victory Lap of the Beach, acknowledging the cheering.

Gumboil bowed towards the Inter-Tribal Friendly Swimming Race Committee. 'My Master greets the Judges, and claims the Victory of being the Last Man Back in this Swimming Contest. And as Last Man Back, according to the Rules, he may make a single demand of the losing Chieftains, Stoick and Bertha.'

Poor Stoick was sitting with his head in his hands. Stoick was not a natural worrier, but he was now terribly concerned about the fate of his son, Hiccup. Now he got to his feet and roared, 'But Hiccup is not back! My son may yet return and claim the prize himself!'

It was a desperate hope, but Stoick was clinging to it. Madguts grinned an unpleasant grin with not enough teeth in it. He whispered in his assistant's ear.

'My Master points out, respectfully,' Gumboil bowed in the direction of Stoick and Bertha, 'that Stoick's son, Hiccup, Bertha's daughter, Camicazi, and the odd looking boy they call Fishlegs, are most likely to have DROWNED in the very first hours of the Competition...'

'*NO!*' bellowed Stoick, with an anger born of fear.

The Inter-Tribal Friendly Swimming Race Committee nodded wisely and sadly to each other. It did seem likely at this point.

'This is true,' admitted the Chief Judge solemnly. 'For Snotface Snotlout here reports that he and Dogsbreath the Duhbrain saw Hiccup and the other two in difficulties. He tried to help them...'

'We did our best,' said Snotlout, sorrowfully and nobly, 'but we were swept away by the force of the current, weren't we, Dogsbreath?'

Dogsbreath grunted, and removed his helmet out of respect for the dead.

'It's a tragedy,' sighed Snotlout. 'Hiccup was like a brother to me...'

Stoick gave a groan of sadness, terrible to hear, and turned away.

'Don't worry, Stoick, my dear chap,' Bertha comforted him awkwardly. 'Camicazi is with him, and, trust me, *she* always turns up all right... *She* could escape from Valhalla itself...'

'And so Madguts demands his prize,' smiled Gumboil silkily. 'And he demands... *the kingdoms of Stoick and Bertha, who should be taken immediately from this beach, and up to the Sky Burial Place on the clifftops to be sacrificed to the Sky Dragons!*'

'Whaaaaaaaat?' roared the Hooligans and the Bog-Burglars in fury. Uproar on the beach.

'But… but… but this is outrageous!' stuttered Bertha. 'He can't ask for *that*!'

'I hope you're not going to go back on your word, Bertha,' Gumboil wagged a warning finger at the apoplectic Bog-Burglar Chief. 'Don't be such a bad sport. I am presuming that if YOU had won, you would have expected Madguts to do YOUR bidding…'

'This is just a Friendly Swimming Race! *We* were only going to ask for Madguts to cross the Sullen Sea in a bathtub with his underpants on his head!' yelled Bertha indignantly.

'More fool you,' smiled Gumboil. Madguts is only asking what *Stoick's* ancestor, Grimbeard the Ghastly, asked of *Madguts'* ancestor, way back in the bad old days…'

Old Wrinkly had been trying to interrupt for some time. He got to his feet and cleared his throat.

'A small technical point, Your Wheeziness,' said Old Wrinkly to the Chief Judge. 'Let me tell again that story from the bad old days, the Saga of Grimbeard the Ghastly and the Swimming Race. Just in case there are some people here who do not know it.'

The saga of
GRIMBEARD THE GHASTLY
and the SWIMMING RACE

Grimbeard the Ghastly was Stoick's great-great-grandfather, a wicked, successful pirate who became the last King of the Archipelago. One day, Murderous the Magnificent challenged Grimbeard the Ghastly to a swimming race, and the two chiefs agreed the winner should be granted a single demand.

So one cold morning they set out from the Western Beach of the Murderous Mountains. Murderous the Magnificent finally swam back to the same beach in seventy-one hours and forty-two minutes, nearly three days in total. His face had swollen to twice the size and his body was so covered in wrinkles he looked like he had been pickled in the brine.

The Hooligan Tribe waited on the beach hoping and hoping for their chief to return. After a week, they accepted that he must have drowned, and conceded the victory to the Murderous Tribe. Murderous the Magnificent claimed the Kingdom of the Archipelago, and that, everybody thought, was the end of the matter. However, three months later, Murderous the Magnificent was conducting a night-time banquet on that very same beach. The highlight of the banquet was the human sacrifice under the stars.

Just before the sacrifice took place, Grimbeard the

Ghastly came staggering out
of the surf. He was barely recognisable.
Half-human, half-monster, with skin like a
dragon, all entwined with seaweed, and he had shark's
teeth around his calves like bracelets.

Grimbeard the Ghastly staggered up the
beach and collapsed. Murderous the Magnificent
raised up his sword to kill what he thought was some
kind of demon... then he saw that the monster was
wearing around its waist Grimbeard the Ghastly's
famous sword, the Stormblade!

The next words that Grimbeard spoke, as he lay
gasping for breath on the sand, can be repeated proudly
by every Hooligan schoolboy, so well-known are they:

Stay your hand, Murderous the Magnificent.
I am no ghost. It is I, Grimbeard the Ghastly, who
have the Greatest Stomach after all. I have survived the
Open Ocean, by the will of Thor, without seeking aid
from float or boat, I am the last man back, and I am come
to claim my Kingdom for the Hooligan Tribe!'

I am afraid that Grimbeard the Ghastly, who
was not a nice man, then insisted as his demand that
Murderous the Magnificent should be sacrificed
to the Sky Dragons. The Annual Inter-Tribe
Swimming Race has been held every year in memory
of this historical event, but over the years it has
become more of a friendly competition.

'There you are, you see!' said Gumboil triumphantly. 'For one hundred years the Murderous Tribe have been waiting for our revenge, and now finally, the time has come, and our pride shall be restored.'

'Stop interrupting!' snapped Old Wrinkly 'Now, Grimbeard was, among other things, a terrible trickster, a practical joker and an all-round cheat. But however he achieved this extraordinary stunt, he returned to this beach, Last Man Back (the Committee might like to check the Sagas for this), exactly THREE MONTHS, FIVE DAYS AND SIX HOURS later! There ARE still three members of the race unaccounted for, namely Hiccup, Fishlegs and the very small Bog-Burglar they call Camicazi. I would propose that if *Grimbeard the Ghastly* could stay out that long, then, technically speaking, *they could too...* so we need to wait three months, three days and eleven hours before Madguts can claim his prize.'

Gasps from the crowd.

The Judges went into a 'Thinking Scrum' to consult upon this matter.

'OK, then,' said the Chief Judge, emerging from the Scrum and banging on the drum. 'HERE IS THE VERDICT of the Inter Tribal Swimming Race Committee. As long as Madguts has stuck to the Rules of the Competition, trickery played within those Rules is a perfectly repectable Viking characteristic.'

Cheers of greedy joy from the Murderous Tribe.

Howls of sadness and fury from the Hooligans and the Bog-Burglars.

'I haven't finished!' cried the Chief Judge. 'Madguts the Murderous is granted temporary custody of Big-Boobied Bertha and Stoick the Vast. And we Judges will stay on the beach to keep watch for the three missing competitors. But the rest of you can go home. And you will return back to this beach exactly three months, five days and six hours from the start of the race. If in that time no one has returned alive from these waters, Madguts the Murderous will be declared Last Man Back, the Berk and Bog-Burglar islands will fall into Murderous hands, and Stoick and Bertha, I am afraid, will be sacrificed to the Sky Dragons...'

The Chief Judge banged his staff upon the ground. And so it was.

The three old Judges sat patiently on the beach, through wind and rain and storm, looking out to sea.

The rest of the Bog-Burglars and the Hooligans sailed sorrowfully back to their islands.

And poor old Stoick and Big-Boobied Bertha were not playing Bashyball in the mud, or supervising the spring shearing, or painting the boats for the summer sailings, as Hiccup had imagined.

They were incarcerated in the deepest and darkest Murderous Cave Dungeons, so cramped and dark that they could barely move a muscle.

There was a tiny barred window in Stoick's dungeon, which had a good view over the Great West Ocean and Stoick would fall asleep sometimes, looking out over this view, and dream that his son was alive, and swimming back to him across the sea. But then he would wake up, and it was nothing but a dream, and all there was was water, water, stretching out for ever, and the cold lonely cry of the seagulls.

15. IT'S A LONG WAY TO AMERICA

Now follows the part of the story in which Hiccup travelled across the Great West Ocean.*

It would take far too long to tell you what happened every minute, every hour, every day.

Thousands and thousands of miles the Great Ship travelled, the puffing fiery furnace sending them skimming across the water far quicker than sails alone. Thousands and thousands of miles across the Ocean, sometimes in sunshine and glass-flat sea and windless skies, sometimes in gales and hurricanes and driving rain, surging up and down on the back of the white-topped waves as if they were aboard a great galloping horse.

Travelling across the Great West Ocean is a VERY long way indeed.

It is indeed *such* a long way, it seemed to Hiccup to be like stepping off the edge of the World and into Forever. And through wind and sun and frost and rain, this Sea-dragon followed the doomed ship, constant as a meteor orbiting the earth, just as if the ship were a planet that had its own particular moon, slowly and predictably circling it.

---

*The Atlantic Ocean, as we now call it.

The Hysterics were still hale and hearty, wolfing down their smoked reindeer with gusto, and washing it down with a nice dose of bull's blood and strong cabbage BEER.

They were in fine, violent spirits, joking with one another, and sometimes going too far, and so the whole deck erupted into fisticuffs, and Norbert had to break up the fights by storming into the centre of the trouble, whirring his axe above his head like the propeller of one of his mad inventions.

The Hysterics sang all day and night long, of their sweethearts at home, of Jellybelly's bright eyes, and Grimhilda's magnificent chin, and fortunes to be made, and blood to be spilt, in the New World called America.

And at night, as they slept, their dreaming minds drew maps of America and each map of this paradise-on-earth was drawn according to their own desires.

To Nutjob it was a place of GOLD, where all his inventions worked like clockwork, and he could rule on a golden throne with a golden crown on his head and a golden axe in one hand.

To lazy little Toothless, it would be a land of FOOD, with small furry animals in such abundance that you barely had to raise a claw to catch them.

And at night, as they slept, their dreaming minds drew maps of America...

You just opened up your little tooth-free jaws, and they elbowed each other out of the way to crowd down your throat, and troop downwards, squeaking, into your fat little stomach.

To Fishlegs, it was a world where nobody tried to make you play Bashyball.

To Camicazi, it was a land full of sword-fights, and kidnaps, and mad, hairy opponents to burgle and tease.

And as for Hiccup…

Why, strange to tell, *Hiccup's* map of America looked a lot like Berk.

Hiccup, Fishlegs and Camicazi often slept at night by the warmth of the ship's chimney, and then spent their days up in their treetop house at the top of the mast, or played upon the rigging, only coming down for Hiccup to read the ticking-thing, or to have a meal.

As the ship puffed south, the weather grew warmer, and they could take off some of their stolen furs and hang them out on the crow's nest.

The Sea-dragon followed them still.

The creaking, clanking, shambolic little wreck of a Machine was held together by bits of old sea rope, and ancient twine. With every revolution of the pedals,

the trumpet-thingy seemed in trembling danger of falling off...

... but by some miracle, the wheels still turned, and it hadn't fallen off...

... *yet*.

Every evening just at sundown, Norbert would summon Hiccup to his tent to read the ticking-thing. There he would be, pacing up and down on the rocking deck in front of his maps, all spread out on the bearskin tablecloth, and as the days went on he grew more and more impatient, clapping his great hands together, and muttering to himself, 'Nearly there now! Nearly there!' before Hiccup told him the reading for the day. Norbert wasn't a very patient man, and this waiting was killing him.

He had a tiny replica of the *American Dream II*, exquisitely made in every detail, but only about eight centimetres high. It had a real working sail, and the writing on the side was so tiny it looked like it had been drawn by a flea. Norbert used his axe to push this boat across the surface of his great map, according to Hiccup's reading of the ticking thing, so that he could see where they might be on the Great West Ocean. Every day it drew nearer and nearer to the great landfall Norbert had drawn on it and called

'AMERICA', until it was now, according to the map, only a day or two's sail away, and Norbert could barely contain his excitement.

Hiccup was very uneasy. He remembered what Norbert had said about how they were only safe for as long as Norbert needed him to read the ticking-thing for him. Now they were so close to America, a nasty look came into Norbert's eye when it rested on Hiccup. Norbert had taken to polishing the dark side of his axe until it gleamed like ebony, whispering to it as if it were a precious pet: 'Not long now my darling... soon you shall be fed...'

Hiccup did not like the sound of this *at all*, and he took the precaution of getting Camicazi to steal them back their weapons. He had a nasty feeling they were going to need them.

So there was a great knot of anxiety in Hiccup's stomach. Especially as he watched the crew while they were having breakfast outside the Cooking Tent the next day. The Hysterics were in an excitable mood, singing their songs with great gusto:

'There's LAND ahead lads, LAND ahead, a LAND of milk and HONEY,

'We'll soon be off these rocking waves and rolling in the MONEY...'

16. LAND AHOY!!!!!!

A storm was brewing.

Ominous clouds were building up in the skies above, like a god with a headache, and the boat was already beginning to rock beneath their feet as the swell grew larger, and the wind picked up.

Suddenly, there was a great flash of lightning that lit up the sky.

Hiccup could see distinctly in that sudden flash the black back of the great Sea-dragon on the horizon.

And *just* as the lightning struck, there was a great gleeful cry of JOY from the lookout on the first mast: 'NUTJOB-LAND AHO-O-O-O-O-O-O-O-Y!!!!!!!!!'

And the Hysterics rushed to the edge of the boat, jostling and trampling and elbowing each other out of the way.

They wanted to be the first to catch a glimpse of that glorious, mythical, land, that mysterious place they called 'America'.

That first sighting was just as wonderful as they could possibly have imagined.

Above them, the storm was breaking, and rain poured down on their heads, as the ship bucked up and down on the back of the plunging waves.

But on the horizon, the long grey smudge of land
that seemed to stretch infinitely from west to east was
bathed in sunshine under the bluest of blue skies.

America.

The land of dreams, it really *did* exist, and in that
wonderful moment, it was just as it should be.

No sooner had Norbert clapped eyes on this
country that he had waited so long, and journeyed so
far, to find, that he drew his axe in order to exact an
old revenge.

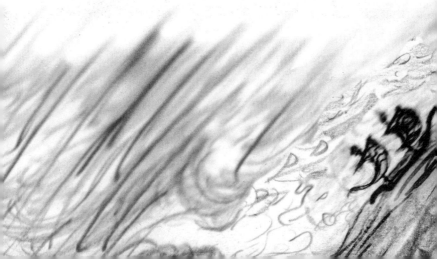

'*Now*, Hiccup Horrendous Haddock the Third,' grinned Norbert the Nutjob, with the light of triumph glowing in his manic eye, 'I have no need of YOU any more... and *now* you will feel the sharp end of the Axe of Doom... PREPARE TO DIE!'

Hiccup leapt up on to a barrel so that everyone could see him. 'DON'T KILL ME JUST BECAUSE I'M A RED-HEAD, NORBERT!' shouted Hiccup as loud as he could.

The Hysterics crowded at the ship's rail turned around.

'What's going on?' asked Verociously Violent, whose hair was a great shock of scarlet, flaming like a fiery furnace.

'What *are* you talking about?' blustered Norbert.

'*NORBERT, HERE, DOESN'T WANT ANY RED-HEADS TO BE LIVING IN THE PROMISED LAND!*' yelled Hiccup. '*HE'S GOING TO KILL US ALL WITH HIS AXE OF DOOM!*'

It just so happened that, by coincidence, quite a lot of the red-headed members of the Hysteric Tribe had suffered at the hands of Norbert's wild temper and his experiments. (For instance, Norbert had sent Verociously Violent and Goggle-eyes the Gory up in the air to try out his Flying Machine experiment TWENTY-SEVEN TIMES, and *every single time*, the Flying Machine had crashed into the sea two minutes after it took off.) So the red-heads drew their swords with an angry rumble of revolt.

For their part, the Hysterics with blond hair had always had a secret feeling of superiority. Now that Norbert had brought it up, what could be better than a whole Tribe of blonds, storming into the Future, hair brighter than the cornfields?

188

So they too drew their swords, and within a couple of seconds, to Norbert's open-mouthed amazement, the entire Tribe of Hysteric Warriors were fighting *each other* as if they were desperate enemies.

It was a terrible battle indeed. Thor's thunder rolled out across the black and angry stormclouds, and great jagged splinters of lightning cracked open the skies and punched down on to the swelling seas all around them. Huge frothing waves spilled over the sides of the boat and across the deck, upsetting the combatants as they fought in the drenching rain.

Camicazi joined Hiccup in fighting Norbert.

'YOU, Norbert,' teased Camicazi, 'have the mental capacity of a jellyfish with a lobotomy. You have the leadership skills of a lemming with a head cold. You couldn't run an Empire larger than my toilet without making a complete dog's breakfast of it... which is a bit of a problem for a dictator...'

Hiccup lunged forward with a Left-handed Heartseeker, and Norbert was so distracted by Camicazi's insults that he only just parried it in time.

And while he was occupied with the parry, Camicazi leapt in and tickled him under the armpits.

'Oooh, nice muscles, Norbert, have you been working out?'

With a howl of fury, Norbert shook her off, and
Camicazi sprang backwards, and ducked his furious
swing of the axe.

'Temper, temper...' she scolded, and so mad
with rage was Norbert that he didn't even
see Hiccup's Twirling Double-Point until it
removed the bottom half of his beard, and
meanwhile, Camicazi sneaked in under his
left arm, and stole the ticking-thing from
out of his pocket, cutting the rope that tied it to
Norbert's wrist.

'Is this yours?' asked Camicazi,
dangling the ticking-thing in front of him.

'Tut, tut, you need to be careful with it, or someone might steal it…'

'Give it here!' roared Norbert, slashing away at her randomly.

'Come and get it…' sang Camicazi, twirling the ticking-thing around her head, and bonking Norbert on the nose with it, before she threw it to Hiccup, who caught it neatly.

The only problem with Camicazi's fighting method was that it tended to make the opponent REALLY REALLY MAD.

Norbert turned as red as a tomato, and LAUNCHED himself at the two young Vikings, howling like a dog.

The swords flashed together, in and out, lunge and parry.

Norbert was a terrifying opponent, with his sword in one hand and his axe swiping in the other.

But even though they were young, as you can see, Hiccup and Camicazi were a formidable fighting duo.

Who knows *what* would have happened, if Toothless hadn't taken it in his head to be helpful.

Toothless grabbed Norbert's big map of America from the table in his Tent, and flapped unsteadily, like a large ungainly moth, over to the scene of the fight. He hovered for a second over Hiccup, Camicazi and Norbert, and then shook his head as he dropped the map, so it spread out nicely as it fell, and floated gently...

... on to the head of Norbert the Nutjob, covering him from the top of his helmet to the bottom of his midriff, like a mysterious lady of the Eastern deserts.

'Oh well done, Toothless!' Toothless congratulated himself, clapping his wings together in an ecstasy of excitement. 'Nice swooping!'

The deck heaved violently on the swell of a wave.

Norbert staggered, trying to regain his balance, but with a map upon his head, he couldn't see where he was going...

He lurched violently to the left... and then wildly to the right, bashing into Red Ronald, still pedalling faithfully away on the Stop-the-Boat-from-Sinking-and-Scare-Away-the-Big-Sea-Creatures Machine, with such force that... Red Ronald... and, most importantly, the MACHINE... the creaky, cranky little Machine that had by some extraordinary chance held together all this way...

... fell over the rim of the boat and into the sea.

There was a mighty pause.

'Oh, Toothless...' moaned Hiccup, with his hands over his eyes.

They were *so close* to America that it had ceased to be a pale grey outline, and was a long swoop of white beach, with great grey waves crashing upon the shoreline, and trees above, and you could even see tiny little mysterious figures moving upon the sand.

But now the Machine was no longer giving out that unbearable high-pitched noise, the Sea-dragon on the horizon – the Sea-dragon that everybody had forgotten about in the heat of the fighting – was *finally* released.

And with a mighty, terrible shriek, it shot towards the boat.

Having regained his balance, Norbert took the Map off his head and blinked twice, first at the spot where the Machine had disappeared over the rim of the boat, then at the Truly Gigantic Dragon moving purposefully towards them.

Nobody was fighting now. Red-heads, blonds, lunatics, *all* had recognised a greater danger, and were crouching down on the deck in fear.

'*HERE IT COMES!*' shouted somebody.

17. THE LEVIATHORGAN STRIKES

The Hysteric nearest to Hiccup fell to his knees, gasping: 'Thor save us!'

All they could see of the Creature were the spines on its back drawing closer and closer in the water.

It was aiming straight for the boat.

But at the very last moment, it changed direction, and swam alongside it. And it was only then that they realised how truly enormous it was.

It was IMMENSE.

As the Dragon passed the boat, it rolled slightly on its side, and one terrible yellow reptilian eye stared at Hiccup, pinpointing him, picking him out. There was a curious expression in that eye, of intelligent humour mixed with the purest fury. It was as if it hadn't forgotten the incident in the Ice Cave, and something in that eye seemed to say, 'You're going to pay for that, boy, and I'm going to enjoy it... You can't get away from me now.'

And then it moved on, muscles rippling, as it swam sinuously as a panther through the water. It swam so close to the boat, that it was almost as if it were showing off how big it was. That long, glorious back with the cruel, primeval spikes, went on, it seemed like, for ever...

Oh for Thor's sake, thought Hiccup, his heart in his mouth, *it must be twice, no nearly* three *times as long as this boat...*

It was a Leviathorgan, all right.

Like all the ancient Sea-dragons, it had probably been alive since the age of the dinosaurs, and it had the look of something dug up from the past. Blackened crustacea festooned its spiny armour like rust. Parts of its body were so encrusted with coral, and trailing with long drifts of seaweed, that it was like a living, moving reef.

The heart-stoppingly huge length of the Leviathorgan swam beside the boat. And then it turned away, and swam on past them, and disappeared below the water, the casual, contemptuous flip of its tail creating such a great white washing powerful wake that it swamped the deck with a wave that covered their knees.

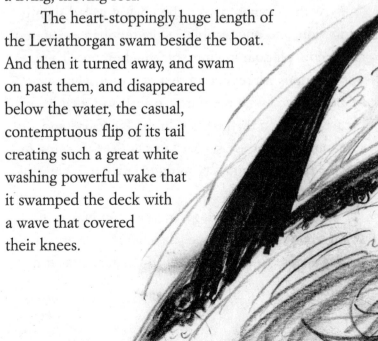

'Where's it gone?'

Many voices called out the same question from the ship.

There had been a look in that Dragon's giant eye which Hiccup had seen in the expression of Toothless when he had cornered something smaller than himself, like a mouse or a rabbit.

We're going To need a bigger boat...

Like cats, dragons have a cruel streak, and they like to play with their food, before they kill it.

'*It's going to play with* US...' thought Hiccup with foreboding. 'Grab on to something on the boat!' he yelled out, winding a rope attached to the mast firmly round his wrist.

'Oh brother,' moaned Fishlegs, as he did the same, 'how did this happen? We just went out for a simple little SWIMMING RACE, is there NO safe activity in this uncivilised world?'

The dragon had dived under the water, and there was no sign of it, just the roaring of the wind, the crashing of the thunder, the drenching rain.

'WHERE IS IT? WHERE'S IT GONE?' someone shouted frantically.

There was an explosion of white water to Hiccup's left, as the Leviathorgan LEAPT out of the sea. It flew right over the boat, and hovered there.

Again, it was almost as if it were showing off how big it was.

It was so enormous that hovering above the great ship's mast, the tips of its great wings *just* grazed the surface of the water as they beat downward on either side.

Its eyes bored down at the Viking ship. Gently

it reached out its gigantic talons, and took hold of the mast of the *American Dream II*, like an eagle grasping a stick.

And then it lifted the entire ship completely clear of the water…

It looked down into the boat to see the reaction of the inhabitants.

Most of them were screaming.

The great Sea-dragon gave the ship a little shake, sending the Vikings inside it catapulting around the deck like marbles… and then it dropped the *American Dream II* back into the water again.

The Monster hung above them still, blotting out the sky, and now it stretched wide its great ancient mouth, far wider than would have seemed physically possible, so that it became a great black cavern, opening up in front of their eyes.

Like an enormous spitting cobra, the Sea-dragon began to hiss.

First a gentle sssssss… getting louder and louder, SSSSSSS, until it built up into such a sinister, angry intensity that it was as if the entire ship were crawling with nests of serpents about to strike. The sound sent goosebumps all over Hiccup's body, and every individual hair on his head stood up as if charged

with static electricity.

The Creature's eyes bulged, its throat worked.

It was looking straight at Hiccup, and instinctively, Hiccup ducked behind the mast.

Something flew through the air, and sunk itself quivering into the wood.

With round, terrified – no, *petrified* – eyes, Hiccup peered round the mast to look at it.

It was the sting of the Leviathorgan.

Hiccup had heard of this in legends. Like a gigantic bee, the Leviathorgan carries stings within its body, but in its throat, inside the fire-hole rather than its abdomen. It can propel these stings from its mouth at astonishing speed, like a rocket launcher.

The sting of a bee is no more than a couple of millimetres long. The sting of a Leviathorgan is roughly the length of a spear.

It had sunk quite eight centimetres into the wood, and remained there, shivering and on fire. It seemed to be made out of some kind of bone as hard as metal, but it was difficult to tell because the flames flickered along its length. A great scarlet-black stain was spreading out on the mast as the poison from the tip leaked out, and Hiccup was just taking off his jacket to smother the flames before they set fire to the mast, when the Leviathorgan entered the water on the other side of the boat.

This time it slapped down its tail with such deliberate force that a wave tipped the boat violently to the left, so much so that the tip of the mast itself nearly reached the water.

Barrels, the Cooking Tent, cauldrons, brooms, Norbert's precious Map Table, his table and chairs, his rugs and his birdcages, Hysterics, forks, pails, and vegetables, all were washed away in a flood of thigh-deep water as the boat dipped so crazily that it almost seemed in peril of tipping over entirely.

Both Fishlegs and Camicazi had lost their grip on what they were holding on to and were washed off by the force of the wave. But the ticking-thing had caught around the mast, and Hiccup remained on the boat.

For a second it seemed as if the boat would up-end completely... and then it righted itself again, and swung back, equally wildly, in the other direction, flinging Norbert back over the edge and spinning him to the centre of the deck.

Again it seemed uncertain that the ship would find its centre of balance, but it rocked back eventually, and rolled drunkenly forward, direction-less now that there was no one at the wheel.

Most of the crew was washed off into the stormy seas.

The deck was ankle-deep in water, stained a bloody red (I'm SORRY for those of you who are squeamish, but it was).

Those crew that remained were either concentrating in putting out the fire on one of the sails before it spread (the Leviathorgan had shot out another flaming sting before it dived back into the sea, and it had passed straight through the end sail, setting it alight), or they were on their knees praying to the great god Thor.

Some, indeed, thought that the Leviathorgan was the incarnation of Thor himself, come down in judgment upon them for their temerity in daring to cross the Uncrossable Waters, and its stings were Thor's lightning bolts raining down upon them.

Many had now abandoned the *American Dream II* as a hopeless cause, a lost ship, and were even now striking out for land as their only hope of survival.

Camicazi and Fishlegs were in the sea.

Fishlegs had got hold of one leg of Norbert's Map Table, which was floating upside-down in the water, and he looked down, and found himself staring at the great black form of the gigantic Leviathorgan swimming just ten metres below him.

'It's all right!' screamed Camicazi. 'It's going for the boat!'

And then they both turned white.

Hiccup was still on the boat.

Hiccup had unfortunately tied the ticking-thing to his wrist a little *too* carefully, with one of Stoick's Foolproof Never-Go-Wrong Slip-Knots, and he was having difficulty *un*tying himself.

'Come on... come on... come on...' he muttered, desperately trying to untangle himself.

'Help me bite it apart, Toothless,' he said, and the little dragon worked at the rope with his sharp little gums, to no avail.

'Hurry up, hurry up!' screamed Hiccup.

'OK, that's it,' said Toothless, folding his wings, and stopping biting. 'Toothless not help the big Mean Master if he be cross with p-p-poor Toothless.'

There was a great crash from below of splintering wood, and the boat rocked crazily, and another crash, and the boat listed to the left and then sank a couple of metres into the water.

OK. that's IT

'*Aaaaghhh!!!! It's holed the boat, it's holed the boat! ABANDON SHIP!!!*' yelled one of the crew, belly-flopping over the side.

'Toothless! Help me!' shrieked Hiccup, scrabbling frantically at the rope, trying to untie it, and only succeeding in making a complete bird's nest of the thing. 'I didn't mean to sound cross, I was just frightened!'

'Is no r-r-reason to be RUDE,' complained Toothless, in a huff. 'And Mean Master still sounding cross.'

'I'm not cross!' squealed Hiccup. 'Get biting! Get biting!'

Toothless wagged a wing at Hiccup. 'First, Mean Master say he *v-v-very* sorry...'

'I'm very sorry!' screamed Hiccup. 'Very, very, very sorry! I couldn't be sorrier!'

'Say, I am a big, wingless idiot and T-T-Toothless the handsomest, cleverest *k-k-kindest* dragon in the WHOLE WORLD...' said Toothless, giggling naughtily.

'I-am-a-big-wingless-idiot-and-Toothless-is-the-handsomest-cleverest-kindest dragon-in-the-whole-world!' gabbled Hiccup.

Norbert was lying in the centre of the deck in a crumpled heap, and for a moment Hiccup hoped, as he frantically worked at the knot, that he was actually, finally, completely dead.

But Norbert seemed to be indestructible. He quivered a little, and then rose like a nightmare from the deck, as he did in so many of Hiccup's dreams, a limping sack of bones and muscles with murder in his eyes.

His clothes were in dripping tatters around him, his face was contorted in fury.

Hiccup could tell from the crazy light in Norbert's eye that he had lost the plot. He no longer cared about escaping the frightful peril of the Creature determined to destroy the boat, or about reaching the American shore, so temptingly close, and yet still so far away.

All he wanted now was the head of Hiccup.

'YOU...' spat Norbert, as he staggered forward, panting hard. 'You, Hiccup Horrendous Haddock the Third are my nemesis... my Curse... If YOU were not in this world I would be a RICH man, counting my American gold... an Emperor perhaps, of the New World... but you and your wretched little flying lizard have foiled my dreams once more. I mean, can't a man

DREAM for Thor's sake? All of my dreams YOU have turned to ashes, time and time again.' Tears of self-pity rolled down Norbert's furious face, as he waded through the knee-deep water.

He staggered forward, his sword raised above his head.

'... and when we get home, I am going to let Toothless have his very own p-p-pet, a dear little rat...' finished Toothless.

'And-when-we-get-home-I-am-going-to-let-Toothless-have-his-very-own-pet-a-dear-little-rat-help-me-Toothless-or-I-am-going-to-DIE!' screeched Hiccup.

At the very last minute, Toothless *finally* unwound the ticking-thing from the mast. Hiccup looked desperately around him as the lightning shook the sky... there was no escape now, nowhere to go but... UP.

In an instant, a Plan popped into Hiccup's mind. The Archipelago was a dangerous place to live, and Hiccup had spent many years coming up with one desperate plan after another, but this was a plan too crazy even to be given the name 'desperate', so let us call it the Suicidal Plan.

Sheathing his sword, the Endeavour, Hiccup began to climb the mast of the *American Dream II*.

18. UP THE MAST OF THE AMERICAN DREAM II

He shinned up the mast like a little monkey, as it reared up and down like a great plunging tree on the back of the waves. He was in terrible danger of being blown off by the shrieking wind that tore at his clothes, and froze his fingers till they nearly lost their grip, but up, and up he climbed.

Norbert halted at the bottom of the mast for a second. He was laughing as he did this, shouting up the mast, 'Where are you going, you small boy? Don't you know you're going to run out of mast, and I shall get you in the end?'

And then he began to climb after Hiccup.

Up and up Norbert climbed in pursuit. He was surprisingly quick, for he had an interesting technique. Every few metres or so he let out a scream of effort as he sank his axe deep into the mast above. And then he hauled himself up, almost entirely with the strength of his upper arms, worked the axe out, and dug it into position a few metres further up.

Hiccup had run out of mast.

He curled the rope of the rigging around his arm

(he was careful not to tie it this time), drew his sword again, and waited for Norbert.

Down in the sea, Fishlegs and Camicazi were watching him, open-mouthed.

'What is he DOING?'

'I think,' said Fishlegs slowly, 'he's going to fight Norbert on the mast.'

Hiccup's fight with Norbert on the mast top has passed into Viking Legend.

Never had a fight been undertaken in such difficult circumstances as these, on top of the rigging and mast of a ship that was rapidly sinking, in the middle of a thunderstorm, and under attack from below by one of the major Monsters of the Deep. Norbert drew his blade with his left hand as soon as he was level with Hiccup, and aimed a great swinging swipe at the boy, which Hiccup parried at the last moment, and the two great swords rang together.

'It's not too late, Norbert,' panted Hiccup, as he parried a Flashburn Fancy-Thrust, and nearly fell off the rigging while doing so. 'Can't we put this off till later? This boat is SINKING.'

As if in response to this statement, the boat gave another lurch downward, and Hiccup was hanging only by one arm for a second before he got his feet back on the ropes, slippery in the drenching rain.

'I've **BEEN** patient!' howled Norbert, slicing through the air with a Double-wristed Heartbreaker. 'Fifteen years stuck on Hysteria! And then two *American Dreams* built and destroyed by **YOU**! Everything was all going to plan, if **YOU** hadn't come along.'

'Well, be fair,' argued Hiccup, steadying himself on the mast as he performed two quick Wristflickers and followed them up with a Grimbeard's Grapple, 'we had to defend ourselves, because you were going to kill us, weren't you?'

'Oh you're always full of excuses,' howled Norbert furiously.

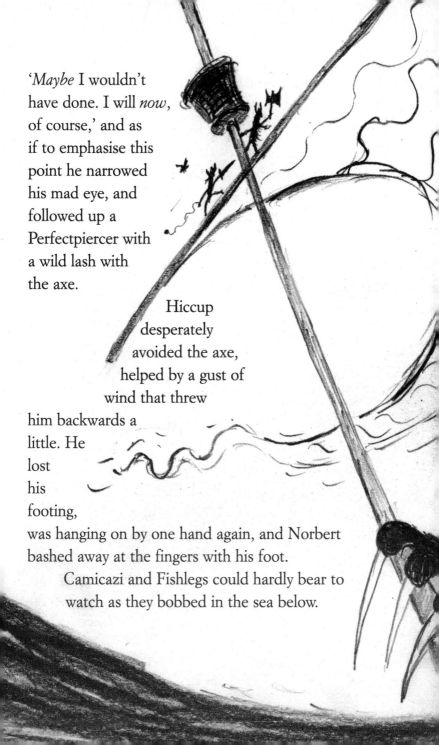

'*Maybe* I wouldn't
have done. I will *now*,
of course,' and as
if to emphasise this
point he narrowed
his mad eye, and
followed up a
Perfectpiercer with
a wild lash with
the axe.

Hiccup
desperately
avoided the axe,
helped by a gust of
wind that threw
him backwards a
little. He
lost
his
footing,
was hanging on by one hand again, and Norbert
bashed away at the fingers with his foot.

Camicazi and Fishlegs could hardly bear to
watch as they bobbed in the sea below.

But Hiccup threw the ticking-thing upwards, and it whipped through the air, and the rope wound itself around the horizontal beam of the mast a little further down. Just at the moment that his hand gave way, he swu-u-ung on the rope, yelling out the Hooligan War Cry, and landed safely a little distance away.

'Oh Bravo, Hiccup!' cheered Camicazi excitedly, 'That was a really cool move.'

Toothless flapping into Norbert's face gave Hiccup the time to regain his footing on the rigging. Hiccup followed up with some graceful Left-Hand Lunges, one of which was so close to disabling Norbert's sword arm that it ripped off the right sleeve.

'I think he's winning, you know, Fishlegs,' chirped Camicazi.

It was an extraordinary sight.

Great crashes of thunder from Thor at his most furious, the distant grey outline of the American shore, the majestic half-sinking ship still pouring steam from its chimney, and then high, high on its mast, the two tiny figures, who had now climbed even higher, and were fighting in the crow's nest...

'Oh for Thor's sake,' gasped Fishlegs, as he clung like a half-drowned little spider to the Map Table. 'What's THAT?'

The Leviathorgan had been repeatedly battering the ship from below, and it must have been very well-made, the *American Dream II*, for it was only now that the hull gave way into splinters, and the head of the great dragon appeared through the deck, screaming in fury, and chomping away at the wood with its fangs. It threw back its head and let out a great roar, shooting three of its stings upwards simultaneously. One of the flaming spears of bone shot straight through the swordfight, the other narrowly missed Norbert's bottom. (*That* would have been uncomfortable.)

As if woken from a dream, Norbert looked down to see the deck destroyed, with the head of the Monster thrusting right through it, and looking up at him and Hiccup.

An appalling stench of long-dead seal and rotting porpoise reeked off its fangs (these large Sea Monsters always smell bad, I'm afraid, owing to their carnivore diet), and the feet of an unfortunate Hysteric crew-member could clearly be seen disappearing down the black cavernous gullet.

Norbert's concentration wavered for a second as he realised he had been carried away by his own anger, and Death was now staring him straight in the face.

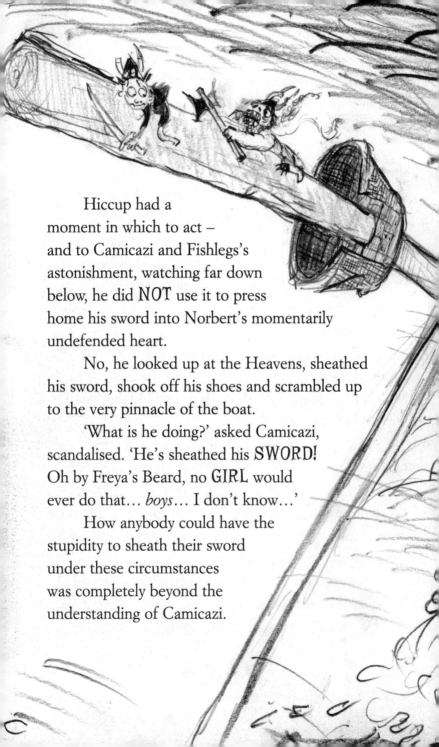

Hiccup had a
moment in which to act –
and to Camicazi and Fishlegs's
astonishment, watching far down
below, he did NOT use it to press
home his sword into Norbert's momentarily
undefended heart.

No, he looked up at the Heavens, sheathed
his sword, shook off his shoes and scrambled up
to the very pinnacle of the boat.

'What is he doing?' asked Camicazi,
scandalised. 'He's sheathed his SWORD!
Oh by Freya's Beard, no GIRL would
ever do that... *boys*... I don't know...'

How anybody could have the
stupidity to sheath their sword
under these circumstances
was completely beyond the
understanding of Camicazi.

Hiccup edged out on to the mast
like a tight-rope walker, the wood cold
beneath his bare feet, his arms flapping outwards
for balance, the wind tearing at his clothes.

He put up his face to the furious storming black
Heavens. 'OK, THOR!' shouted Hiccup. 'THIS IS
YOUR CHANCE TO SHOW ME, ARE YOU ON
MY SIDE, OR ARE YOU NOT?'

The small boy wobbled, teetered, on the mast of
the sinking ship, with his arms stretched up and out, it
wasn't quite clear whether for balance or in prayer to
the storming skies above.

For one second, the boat seemed to stop sinking.
The Leviathorgan, with its paw hauling its great body
up the mast, greedy jaws a-gape, froze like a statue,
even the storm seemed to ease for a second.

'Norbert!' shouted Hiccup above the howling
of the wind. 'If it is, as you say, all my fault, then Strike
me Down Now, for then at least one of us shall die
happy!'

Another pause.

And then everything happened very quickly.

Norbert hauled himself up high on the pinnacle.

Hiccup was right, at least he would go to Valhalla in a moment of triumph.

He raised the Axe of Doom above his head with a scream of victory, ready to bring it down on the unarmed boy with the outstretched arms and upturned head. The air above fizzed with electric energy, crackling, bursting, searching, *seeking* for a path down to the sea.

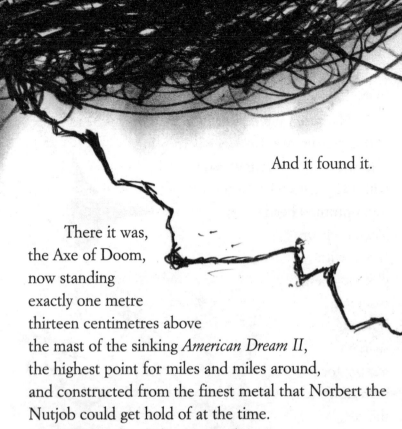

And it found it.

There it was,
the Axe of Doom,
now standing
exactly one metre
thirteen centimetres above
the mast of the sinking *American Dream II*,
the highest point for miles and miles around,
and constructed from the finest metal that Norbert the
Nutjob could get hold of at the time.

The perfect lightning conductor.

A crooked bolt of tremendous lightning jagged
down from the clouds, and struck the blackened point
of the axe.

The second before it struck, Hiccup's toes left
the mast as he sprang off and out in a (not quite
perfect) swallow dive.

The lightning struck the Axe of Doom, and
three-hundred-thousand volts of electricity ran
sparkling down the arm of Norbert the Nutjob,

bristling down the mast, and straight through the body of the Leviathorgan.

Sparks flew from Norbert's nose and jumped crazily off the wood of the mast, setting it alight, and frazzled around every spiny tip of the Leviathorgan's jerking body, in a beautiful impromptu firework display.

The body of Norbert the Nutjob fell from the peak and down, down into the sea.

The Leviathorgan crashed down too, through the hull in another cascade of water and wood splinters. And then **DOWN** went the *American Dream II*, and down in style, with her sinking mast in flames.

Down went the largest, most technically sophisticated boat that a Viking has ever built, already turning into a wooden skeleton, a ghost, as she sank slowly through the cold, grave fathoms to the sea-bed below. And nestled within her in the darkness, as if she were his coffin, was the dead body of the Leviathorgan.

It had tried to eat the boat, but ended up
with the boat eating it, its white picked-
clean bones sleeping for ever more in
the belly of the ghost ship on the
sea-bed. And a boat like that
has never been made again
by the Vikings, as far
as I know.

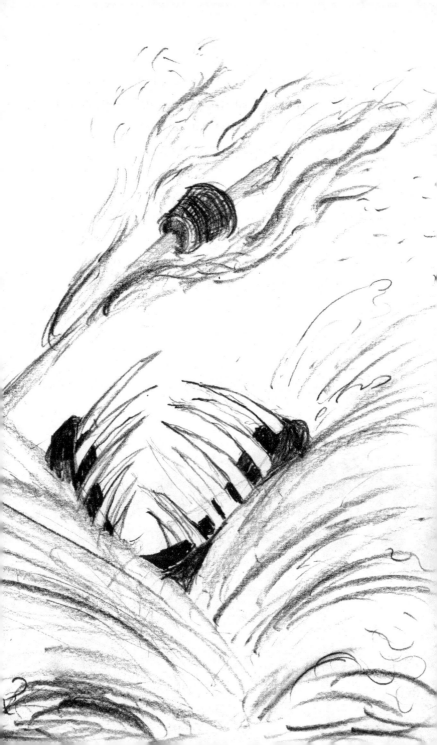

Norbert the Nutjob may have been a maniac, but lunacy and genius are very close together, and it had to be admitted, he was a great Dreamer.

Perhaps the inventor-madmen of the Future will dream its like again.

But for now it was no more, and down it went, the death of Norbert's Dream, the sinking of all his hopes.

And, incidentally, the only way they had of getting back to the Archipelago.

19. KEEP KICKING, IT'S A LONG SWIM HOME

What happened to Hiccup?

As I said, he jumped off the mast in a not-very-perfect swallow dive. Toothless dived after him, folding back his wings. It was a long way down, and by the time Hiccup reached the breath-stoppingly cold sea, he was moving at quite a speed.

Momentum took Hiccup quite a way downward, and as he resurfaced, he hit his head on a cauldron, which was slowly sinking down to the bottom. Hiccup spat out water, gasping and confused, not sure where he was, or *who* he was or what was going on. Blood was pouring into his eyes, and he fainted.

Toothless let out a scream of alarm to Camicazi and Fishlegs, and dived down to pull his Master up so that his face was out of the water. Camicazi immediately set out in her sprawling crawl to try and help, but she was some distance from where Hiccup had landed, so she was never going to be able to reach him in time. Fishlegs, on the other hand, was very close.

As Hiccup disappeared under the water for the second time, Fishlegs let go of the table, and splashed haphazardly across to his friend.

225

He hauled Hiccup up, still unconscious, and heaved him a couple of metres or so to the relative safety of the floating table.

'Oh for Thor's sake, oh for Thor's sake… is he all right?' asked Camicazi as she reached them. Hiccup was sprawled floppily on his back, still breathing but with his eyes closed, and one arm trailing into the water.

'I don't know…' replied Fishlegs anxiously. 'He's still alive, but he's been knocked out. I think he hit his head on something under the water.'

'We need to get him out, *fast*,' cried Camicazi. 'and get him warm.'

The storm had passed as suddenly as it arrived, and was already moving on to the land called America, leaving chaos in its wake. It was as if an angry god had turned the ship upside-down, shaken out its contents, and tossed the boat to the depths. All around them, the surviving Hysterics were striking out for the American shore, swimming around the myriad of objects floating in the waters.

Saucepans, chairs, tables, hammocks, chessboards, stools, fishing equipment, pairs of trousers: Norbert had been very ambitious about the amount of STUFF that he was taking to America.

And they were all now strewn about the waves, and would be washed up for many years on those white beaches, and I wonder what the native American peoples made of them when they found them.

Camicazi tried to pull the table towards the land, but Fishlegs was wondering what the little figures walking about on the beaches would make of THEM when they swam up the shore.

It is one thing to turn up in a new country in all the pomp and circumstance of a great big boat, heavily armed, and laden down with good things to eat and trade. It is quite a different thing, as poor refugees throughout history will tell you, to turn up practically naked, unarmed, defenceless and with nothing in your hands.

As strangers from an alien nation, would they be greeted with interest and mercy? Or would they be greeted with fear, and a hail of arrows?

'No!' cried Fishlegs, pulling in the other direction. 'No! I think we should swim over there!' And he pointed out to sea.

'Are you out of your tiny little mind?' asked Camicazi. 'The Archipelago is thousands and thousands of miles away across the Great West Ocean. You think we're going to SWIM to it?'

'No, of course not,' gasped Fishlegs, accidentally swallowing a big gulp of sea-water. 'But I think I can see the outline of a boat on the horizon… I just have this really strong feeling it wouldn't be a good idea for us to land on that beach…'

The faint noise of shouting coming from the beach in question seemed to underline that feeling.

'Oh I don't know,' shivered Camicazi, faint with weariness and cold.

'OK, let's swim out a little further, we can always change our minds,' she agreed.

So they began to swim away from the beach.

'But *you* can't live in the ocean! Humans haven't got gills!' Stormfly pointed out.

Toothless fanned Hiccup's face with his wings, to try and get him to wake up. 'We n-n-need you M-m-master! These h-h-humans don't know what they're doing!'

The thing is, after a while, as they swam out further and further, it became clear that they couldn't necessarily change their minds.

They were so weak with cold and exhaustion that they weren't swimming fast at all, particularly because between the two of them they had to push the table along the water and over the waves. And there must have been a strong, unseen current beneath them, for they were moving out to sea at a very rapid rate. And the sails that Fishlegs thought he had seen seemed to vanish in the sea-mist as they swam towards them,

until Fishlegs began to doubt he had
ever really seen them at all.

They didn't speak of it, though they both knew
what was happening.

They were too frozen and too tired to speak, and
they needed all their energy to keep kicking.

'Keep kicking... keep kicking... keep kicking...'
Fishlegs muttered.

Strange how a story sometimes seems to end just
how it started, in a circle.

They had set out, swimming away from the beach
at the bottom of the Murderous Mountains, many
weeks before.

And now here they were, swimming out into the
very same Ocean, from the opposite direction, and
from a very different shore.

After a while, the land behind them had been
covered by mist. And they had become just another
strange floating object in an alien environment, two
Viking children pushing a table with another child's
body on it across a vast and lonely Ocean.

Above them hovered two dragons, wings spread
wide and tossed up by the wind.

There was still quite a swell, so they were riding up the waves, and then having to hold their heads up high as the wave washed over them, until they dropped down and were picked up by another one. Their feet were so cold they could barely kick now, and they had lost all feeling in their arms.

Toothless tried to help by catching fish and offering it to them, but poor humans, they are so helpless, they didn't even seem to want to eat it.

After about half an hour Camicazi said through numb and frozen lips, 'You DID learn to swim there, though, didn't you? You pulled Hiccup out without holding on to anything. I *told* you you could do it!'

'I did didn't I?' gasped Fishlegs. 'I didn't even think about it.' He gave a shaky laugh. 'Well, *this* has all been worth it then, hasn't it? What a way to learn to swim!'

Camicazi started laughing, hysterically and faintly, and then she said, 'Maybe we should go back now.'

'In a little while, perhaps,' said Fishlegs. 'Keep kicking... keep kicking...'

After another twenty minutes, Camicazi said, 'I think I might have a little nap, I'm feeling very tired...'

'All right then,' said Fishlegs, 'We'll just

sleep a little while, and then we'll carry on.'

The two dragons fluttered down, and landed on two of the table legs, sitting up straight and stiff like two guardian angels on a bedstead. The two Vikings laid their tired frozen heads on the table, and Fishlegs was just dropping off when he saw through half closed eyes…

… a ship, surprisingly close, looming out of the mist.

'Over here,' he whispered, his voice-box so cold that noise could barely come out of it, and then a bit louder, and dragging himself up on to his elbows, 'OVER HERE!'

He shrugged off his waistcoat, and half-stood up on the table, waving the waistcoat over his head. 'OVER HERE! OVER HERE! OVER HERE! Camicazi, wake up, there's a ship, there's a ship!'

'Oh go away and leave me to sleep…' muttered Camicazi, not opening her eyes. 'It isn't morning time yet.'

The people on the ship seemed to hear the shouting, for there were cries in a strange language from aboard, and it moved towards them, nearer and nearer.

'Wake up, Camicazi, wake up! There really *is* a ship!' cried Fishlegs. 'In fact, more than one ship!'

And when Camicazi opened her eyes, there they were, seven ships, and standing on the front of the deck of the first one, straight and tall as a figurehead, and holding aloft a flare in her right hand so they could see through the mist…

… was Bearcub's Grandmother.

'I hope we're not too late,' she said. And then she saw Hiccup's prone body on the table. 'But I see we may be,' she said, with sorrow, but also perhaps a certain amount of gloomy satisfaction.

There were seven Wanderer ships that had followed the *American Dream II* across the Great West Ocean. Wanderers are the best trackers in the world, so they are good people to have following you.

They had known they were getting close to the *American Dream II* for the past hour, because they had begun to pick up a trail of the wreckage strewn in the sea. Candlesticks, barrels of vegetables and jars of beer, chairs, oars, maps, cups, swords and saucepans – all the mad remains of a doomed voyage.

They picked up all that they could find, in case it would be useful or valuable, because Wanderers are not a wealthy people, and this was riches to them.

One of the ships had even retrieved Norbert's defective Flying Machine, and balanced it on the back of its deck, so that it looked as if it were about to take off into the sky.

Bearcub's Grandmother had begun to think that Hiccup had drowned, or landed on the shore of America, when they spotted the floating table in the distance.

It turned out that Bearcub's Grandmother was a surprisingly good nurse, for one so good at Cursing. She was much better at it than Old Wrinkly, the doctor of the Hooligan Tribe, whose cures and potions of seagulls' droppings mixed with spider webs often made you feel somewhat worse than you did before you went to see him.

A couple of hours and some of Bearcub's Grandmother's medicine later, and Hiccup's eyes opened, to see the faces of Fishlegs, Camicazi, the Stormfly, Toothless, Bearcub and Bearcub's Grandmother looking down at him.

'I thought you had left us,' said Hiccup to Bearcub's Grandmother, in surprise.

'Why did you think that?' snapped Bearcub's Grandmother. 'We could not follow you in those titchy little landing-boats, we had to fetch some proper ships. We Wanderers are a people of our word, unlike some other people I can mention.'

20. THE TICKING THING STARTS TO TICK LOUDER

Again, I will not weary you with the details of the long journey home, the dragons they saw, the storms they survived, the perils of the crossing, or we would be here for ever.

Every day, Hiccup checked the ticking-thing. As they grew closer and closer and closer to home, their hearts were lifting with excitement.

But something had begun to worry Hiccup. It was something that Old Wrinkly had said on the beach, on the day of the Inter-Tribal Friendly Swimming Race. He had told Hiccup that he had to be back within three months, five days and six hours.

Now, why would Old Wrinkly say that?

It may seem obvious to you, dear Reader, for you know all the facts, but it never occurred to any of *them* that the Race they had been participating in was either particularly important in itself (it was only a Friendly, as far as they were concerned, after all, and there were always Competitions going on in the Archipelago), or that the Race could still be *going on* all that time later.

So Hiccup didn't know why Old Wrinkly would say such a precise time. And it was concerning him, because according to his reading of the ticking-thing, they had now been gone for three months, four days and thirteen hours, and they were still at least two days' sailing away from the Archipelago.

'I don't know why you're worrying about this,' said Fishlegs, who was in a hugely happy mood now they were nearly home. 'It probably didn't mean anything at all. You know Old Wrinkly, he's not that great a soothsayer, and he's sometimes a bit batty.'

'But what if it *did* mean something?' insisted Hiccup. 'What if Old Wrinkly had seen what was going to happen to us... he knew we weren't going to come back that day, didn't he? And look, we're nearly coming in at exactly the time he said, it's just that we're going to be a bit late, and he *particularly* told me not to be late...'

The next day, Hiccup was even more worried, and the ticking-thing began to tick louder, as Old Wrinkly had said it would.

TICK-TOCK-TICK-TOCK-TICK-TOCK.

'Look!' said Hiccup anxiously. 'That means there's only six hours left, and even though it's a very windy day, we're at least...' he checked the ticking-thing, 'TWENTY-FOUR-hours' sailing distance away... we're going to be late!'

239

'Late for *what*?' asked Fishlegs in exasperation. 'There's nothing we can do about it, anyway, and Old Wrinkly probably didn't mean anything when he said it.'

Hiccup fiddled and fiddled with the ticking-thing as he worried, and the back of it fell open, and for the first time he noticed, along with the little delicate moving wheels on the inside, there was a tiny little inscription. Two letters. G.G.

Hiccup's heart beat a little quicker, for he had seen those letters before, and he knew what they stood for.

Grimbeard the Ghastly.

Hiccup had assumed that this ticking-thing had been made by Norbert's father, Bigjob, and he had always felt a little guilty about stealing it from Norbert.

But it seemed that Bigjob had perhaps stolen it himself.

For this ticking-thing, surely, belonged to the Heir of Grimbeard the Ghastly, and the Heir to Grimbeard the Ghastly was...

... Hiccup.

And now he was *absolutely* sure that there was a precise reason for the time that Old Wrinkly had given him. He did not yet know what the reason was, but he was certain that somehow there was some kind of pattern to it that he did not yet understand.

Some way in which everything interconnected, like the little tiny wheels revolving in the instrument in front of him.

Six hours.

TICK-TOCK-TICK-TOCK-TICK-TOCK
went the ticking-thing, a little louder still.

They were never going to get there in six hours... *by boat.*

Hiccup looked up and his eye caught Norbert's defective Flying Machine, salvaged from the sea by the prudent Wanderers, and now lashed to the figurehead of one of the other Wanderer boats.

There was a very strong wind today.

Hiccup knew from the time that he had spent in a Roman Observation Balloon (it's a long story, don't ask)* that flying was much quicker than sailing.

If only that Flying Machine actually **WORKED**.

Fishlegs saw what Hiccup was looking at, and guessed what he was thinking. 'Oh no, Hiccup, oh, seriously, you have got to be JOKING! Remember how many times they tried that thing out on the journey? And how many times it fell out of the sky like a stone? That Flying Machine *doesn't work.*'

---

*Please read *How to Speak Dragonese.*

'We thought the Stop-the-Boat-from-Sinking-and-Scare-Away-the-Big-Sea-Creatures Machine didn't work, didn't we?' Hiccup pointed out. 'And we were wrong.'

'But we're so close now... so close... and so **ALIVE** which is the important thing,' gasped Fishlegs. 'what is the **POINT** of risking it all right now, after all that we've been through, when we're so very nearly there? No, I'm putting my foot down this time, Hiccup, I can't let you do it...'

TICK-TOCK-TICK-TOCK-TICK-TOCK-TICK-TOCK went the ticking-thing.

21. THE END OF THE SWIMMING RACE

On the windy clifftops of the Murderous Mountains stood the proud figures of Stoick the Vast and Big-Boobied Bertha, their arms in chains, surrounded by Murderous Warriors. They were too dignified to show fear. They would show Madguts the Murderous how bravely a Chieftain could die. Before them was the Sky Burial Place, where they would be strapped down and left, helpless, for the Sky Dragons to attack them. Nothing would be left of their remains.

Above their heads, the Sky Dragons were already massing in their hundreds, with shrieking, hungry vulture cries.

Down on the beach, the Tribes of Hooligan and Bog-Burglar stood, depressed and silent, holding burning flares in their hands, looking up at the silhouettes of their Chiefs on the clifftops.

The deaths of their Chieftains were not the only things at stake here for the two Tribes. Madguts was about to take over their lands. The Hooligans and Bog-Burglars had packed up all their belongings, and loaded them into their own ships standing in the Harbour. These ships were piled high with every

243

possession they owned:
favourite swords and armour,
stools and clothing,
clucking hens and pigs
and goats.

The Hooligans
had never intended
to settle on Berk in the
first place. Berk was not the
most comfortable, the most
luxurious, the most civilised place
to live in the world. It was a funny,
boggy, shaggy little heap of heather and
rock, where the wind buffeted so strongly
that you might as well be on the sea in a
ship, and when it wasn't raining it was often
snowing.

But Berk was where they had grown up,
where they met their sweethearts and brought up
their children, and when it came down to it, they
found that they didn't want to leave.

So they stood there, sunk in the profoundest melancholy.

The sun was going down on this day, and Old Wrinkly's big sand-timer was running out of sand, and his complicated candlesticks were running down to little stubs, marking the Final End to the Competition. The three Judges sat solemnly at the table.

Three months, five days, three hours and twenty-*four* minutes... Three months, five days, three hours and twenty-*five* minutes...

*   *   *   *   *   *   *

Norbert's defective Flying Machine worked rather better than Fishlegs had expected.

But he hadn't expected *much*, it had to be said.

Fishlegs and Camicazi insisted on going in the Machine with Hiccup, Camicazi because it was the kind of crazy thing she particularly enjoyed, Fishlegs because despite all the complaining he wasn't going to desert Hiccup, who was the closest thing to family that Fishlegs had.

The Wanderers had to haul the Machine up to the top of the mast so they could take off in it, and Bearcub's Grandmother predicted Doom and

246

Destruction would be the outcome. 'Vikings – they're all mad... even the small ones...'

But Doom and Destruction did not follow – not immediately, at least.

It was a very windy day, and when the Wanderers let go of the Machine, lift-off was instantly successful. The wind caught underneath the wings and launched the Machine almost vertically up into the air, like a kite.

'Wahooooooooo!' cried Camicazi, as they soared, legs dangling, hair blown back in the wind, up and up into the big blue sky.

'If Thor meant humans to fly, he'd have given them wings,' recommended the Stormfly, swooping alongside them in an amused way.

The wind was strong, the young Vikings were light, and they quickly left the seven boats with the cheering, waving Wanderers on them far, far behind. They were heart-stoppingly high.

Hiccup had flown on the backs of dragons before, but never at this height.

They were so far up in the sky that it was difficult to see how fast they were flying, apart from the marker of the little boats, now only specks way behind them in the distance.

It was cold up there, so cold that Hiccup was glad that they had tied themselves to the Machine, because their fingers were so numb they might have fallen out, and the sea was a very long way down.

And they were up there for such a long time, that after a while, even Fishlegs began to feel that they weren't going to plummet out of the sky like a stone, and opened up his eyes to look about him, at the blue above and below, stretching out for ever.

TICK-TOCK-TICK-TOCK-TICK-TOCK-TICK-TOCK went the ticking-thing, getting louder and louder and more insistent with every passing moment. *I hope we're going to make it...* thought Hiccup.

And after a long, long time, a grey smudge appeared on the horizon before them, and Hiccup shouted over the wind, and pointed towards it, and as it slowly became larger and greener, it was clear that it was the Murderous Mountains.

'HOW ARE WE GOING TO GET *DOWN?*' shouted Fishlegs, because they were still so high that he had a sudden vision of them sailing right over the Archipelago and beyond. But a sudden SNAP! from one of the wings of the Machine above them provided the answer to Fishlegs's question.

The Machine lurched violently to the right.

They lost height with such rapidity that Hiccup's stomach lurched and his ears popped. And Norbert's defective Flying Machine folded up its wings, and plunged in a nose-dive towards the sea.

'AAAAAAAAAAAaaaaaaaaagggggghhhhhh!' screamed Hiccup, Fishlegs, and Camicazi.

*   *   *   *   *   *   *

Madguts the Murderous strode up and down the beach, his cape whirling, Gumboil trotting after him, rubbing his black-gloved hands together.

In fifteen minutes, the Murderous Tribe would

have the revenge for which they had waited a hundred years...

Fourteen minutes... whispered the Judges together, staring at the sand-timers.

Thirteen minutes...

On the stroke of thirteen minutes, Old Wrinkly thought he caught a sound coming from out to sea. He shielded his eyes from the rays of the setting sun with one gnarled and wrinkled hand, and cupped the other behind his ears. Was it just his imagination playing tricks on him? Was it just the beat of his old heart making the sound that he so longed to hear?

For the first time in three months the old man got to his feet, his ancient legs shaking as he leant heavily on his staff. He stumbled forward in the sand, straining, longing, *willing* it to be the sound he wanted it to be... and there it was.

Coming from out of the sea, soft but getting louder every second.

TICK-TOCK-TICK-TOCK-TICK-TOCK

To the astonishment of the watching crowds, the old man let out a cracked old laugh, and began to dance in the sand on his bent old legs, his clothes flapping around him like a scarecrow doing a jig.

He's really lost it… they thought, as Old Wrinkly bustled back to the Judges' Table, his eyes now brimful of merriment and excitement.

And then came a shout from the clifftops.

Stoick shouted out something, and pointed, and the crowd could not hear what he was saying, but they looked where he was pointing, towards the long rolling waves coming in from the West. There was nothing there but the path of the setting sun lighting up the tops of the long waves rolling in from the west.

But then there came a cry, from Nobber Nobrains maybe, 'Look! Over there!'

And there, distinctly, far into the bay, were three little heads bobbing in the waves.

'What is this?' snarled Gumboil, screwing up his eyes to try and see what they were looking at out there in the water. 'Those are just SEALS.'

'Seals with horns?' asked Gobber the Belch, with hope rising in his chest.

'Deer, then,' argued Gumboil.

But as the little heads swam nearer and nearer it became clear that they were not deer. Those were VIKING helmets on their heads, and hovering protectively above them, were the distinct shapes of two small hunting-dragons. And as they came nearer

252

and nearer still, Old Wrinkly cried out: 'Remember!
They must land here unaided!'

His warning was unnecessary for it was as if the
crowd had been turned to stone, so dumbfounded
were they.

The three figures swam closer and closer until
they got into their depth, and then they put their feet
down on the sand of the Archipelago, and they waded
waist high through the crashing waves.

Hiccup, Camicazi and Fishlegs staggered out
of the water of the Great West Ocean, exactly three
months, five days, five hours, and fifty-eight minutes
after they had entered it.

They were totally bewildered to find everybody
on the beach, flares in their hands, apparently waiting
for them, and absolutely silent and stunned.

They had entered the Ocean all that long, long
time ago, a laughing-stock. The smallest contestants
in the Race, jeered at, pointed at, humiliated and
embarrassed. Now the same crowd that had laughed
them so uproariously into the water, greeted them with
awed, wide-eyed wonder and amazement.

Slowly, the huge adults on the beach removed
their helmets as they passed, the ultimate sign of
respect. They fell back in wonder at the soft footprints

in the sand. They murmured their astonishment as great hairy forearms were raised in admiring salute.

It was the proudest moment in Fishlegs's life. He had left this very beach an object of ridicule, unable to swim and wearing those ridiculous armbands. Now all those who had laughed had watched him as he swam, entirely unaided, up the whole depth of the bay. Even though he was so tired he could barely put one foot in front of another, his back was straight, his head held high.

As he passed he heard one Hooligan whisper to a Bog-Burglar... 'That's Fishlegs, there, the one on the right...' in a tone of recognition and admiration.

A proud moment for Fishle...

Imagine that, for a boy used only to being ignored or laughed at!

Fishlegs, Hiccup and Camicazi had equalled Grimbeard the Ghastly's record, but they did not look like they had spent the time pickled in the sea. Their hair was so stiff with salt water it stuck out like broom-brushes. Their faces tanned dark brown. They were a little taller maybe. (Well, it *had* been three months, and pre-teens can grow a great deal in three months.)

They were, without question, this skinny, unlikely threesome, the last three competitors to return alive to the Archipelago.

The Last Men (and Woman) Back.

Hiccup staggered forward to the Judge's Table, too tired to ask questions, almost too tired to think, the ticking-thing dragging behind him in the sand,

TICK-TOCK-TICK TOCK-TICK-TOCK TICK-TOCK...

He stopped at the Judges' Table, and wound the rope of the ticking-thing around his wrist, placing the ticking-thing carefully before the dumbfounded Committee.

Softly, the two small hunting dragons folded their

wings, and landed on the Table their eyes fixed on the
ticking-thing in the centre.

TICK-TOCK
TICK-TOCK...

... and the alarm on the ticking-thing finally went
off, in a peal of tiny clockwork bells, ringing to the
sound of the Hooligan National Anthem.

A typical Grimbeard the Ghastly touch.

You had to admit it, the guy did have STYLE.

Old Wrinkly reached out and turned it off.

'I wasn't late,' said Hiccup.

'No,' said Old Wrinkly. 'You were just in time.'

The Bog-Burglars and Hooligans were so amazed
they just stood there, eyes open wide as saucers,
staring at them.

Madguts was looking like a thundercloud.

'I do not believe this!' spluttered Gumboil.
'Madguts does not believe it... These are just
CHILDREN... and quite odd looking children at that.
They can't possibly be the LAST MEN BACK.'

Nobody could believe it. Snotlout was lost for
words. How did Hiccup DO it? Yet again, it had
seemed certain that he had kicked the bucket, and yet

here he was, turning up very much alive and in a horribly glorious manner. Even that weed Fishlegs seemed to have somehow taught himself to swim.

'Yes, well they're *not* the Last Men Back are they, unless they are able to take the Oath that they did not seek aid by Float or Boat,' Snotlout pointed out meanly, so eaten up with jealousy that he spoke without thinking.

Snotlout's own father, Baggybum the Beerbelly, shouted: 'Shut up Snotlout!' and there were cries of 'Shame!' and 'Whose side are you on, Big Nose?' And even the Murderous Tribe booed and hissed him, for nobody likes a traitor to their Tribe. Snotlout turned a bright and unattractive red, and muttered sullenly, 'I was only *saying…*'

'Yes, as Snotlout so *kindly* reminds us,' said Old Wrinkly, shooting Snotlout a venomous look, 'for any of you to be declared Last Man Back, you have to take the Oath. Can you take the Oath?'

Hiccup, Fishlegs and Camicazi at last realised the significance of what was happening. They looked up at the clifftops, at the long line of little figures standing silent below the wheeling, shrieking Sky Dragons. They looked around at the serious, intent faces of the Tribesmen. They looked at each other.

Well… the Oath said that you were not allowed to 'seek aid' from Float or Boat.

None of them had *asked* to be kidnapped by Norbert the Nutjob. And only Fishlegs and Camicazi had 'sought aid' from the Wanderers, to take them back to the Archipelago. Hiccup had been knocked out, unconscious at the time, not in a condition to seek aid from anyone. And a Flying Machine was neither a Float nor a Boat.

So, *technically speaking*, Hiccup COULD take the Oath.

Fishlegs and Camicazi pushed Hiccup forward.

Hiccup put up his left hand.

Total silence from the crowd.

'I solemnly swear by this my sword-arm,' said Hiccup, 'that I did not seek aid by Float or Boat… I did not plan to win this Race by trickery or deception… and that any assistance I received was by the favour of Fortune, and the gracious will of the great god Thor.'

The crowd erupted with joy.

The Chief Judge signalled to the Murderous Warriors on the clifftops, and reluctantly they let Bertha and Stoick the Vast free of their chains, and the two Chieftains walked proudly down the cliff-paths to the beach, heads held high.

Cheers rang out along the bay, and 'SILENCE!' yelled Old Wrinkly, bursting with pride, for it is not every day that a grandson returns to you from out of the water, a Competition is won, and a prophecy is fulfilled.

(And he was rather proud of his soothsaying skills on this occasion – Old Wrinkly's soothsaying did not always turn out this well.)

He turned his grandson around to face the crowd.

'He did not seek aid by Float or Boat,' cried Old Wrinkly solemnly in his ancient old quavering voice. 'And therefore I declare that the winner of this Competition, and the Last Man Back, to be... *HICCUP HORRENDOUS HADDOCK THE THIRD!*'

Old Wrinkly held Hiccup's arm up in the air victoriously.

'This is preposterous!' spluttered Gumboil. 'This is impossible! He can't have done it! He must have cheated!'

Gumboil found himself grabbed around the throat and lifted up in the air, his little legs dangling like a frantic beetle.

'Are you suggesting, that *MY* ancestor, Grimbeard the Ghastly, and, more importantly, *MY SON AND HEIR*, Hiccup Horrendous Haddock the Third, are *LIARS?* spat Stoick the Vast, pressing his face menacingly into Gumboil's.

'Erm... no... not exactly...' gargled the strangled Gumboil, his voice squeaking like a five-year-old.

Oh, how the Hooligans and Bog-Burglars cheered then, throwing their helmets up into the air, and clapping Hiccup and Camicazi and Fishlegs on the back, and Bertha and Stoick hugged them hard, and they all made ready to leave for their boats moored in Wrecker's Bay, because, frankly, they had had enough of the Murderous Mountains to last them a very long time indeed.

'Wait!' called the Chief Judge, the sad little Bashem-Oik. 'Before you go, there is just one more thing,' he said. 'And that is the question of the demand of the Last Man Back. According to the Oath declared by all, the Last Man Back may demand a request that cannot be denied from the Chieftain of the opposite Tribe.'

The cheers died down and the mood darkened. And Madguts had gone very silent and still, as he realised his trick had turned on himself, and he had played into his Enemy's hands. Stoick's grin turned to a thunderous frown, Bertha's hands were on her hips.

'What is your request, Hiccup? You can ask anything, anything at all.'

Madguts the Murderous had turned rather white, and he fiddled nervously with his sword. He did not have a leg to stand on, and he knew it. He only had himself to blame for the situation in which he now found himself.

The faces of the Bog-Burglars and the Hooligans were hard and set and seeking Revenge. They drew their weapons and tapped them on their thighs, and the air was filled with menace. Up on the clifftops the Sky Dragons circled. *They* didn't care WHO they ate.

'What will it be, Hiccup? What is your demand?' asked Old Wrinkly.

Hiccup thought for a long, long time, looking out over the waters.

The thing about history is that it has this nasty habit of repeating itself. If he did to Madguts what Madguts was intending to do to *them*, well, Madguts would only be getting his just desserts. But then the cycle of revenge would just start anew. In a hundred years' time, did he want Madguts' Heir and his own Heir to be playing out the same tragedy all over again?

At some point it might be a good idea to say goodbye
to the Bad Old Days...

'I demand,' said Hiccup slowly, 'that Chief
Madguts the Murderous should sing a love song
at the next Thing* while dressed as an ickle pretty
shepherdess.'

A pause. Everybody looked at Stoick to see what
his reaction would be.

For a moment Stoick remained purple with fury,
the angry flush of the Blood-Rage still engorging his
face, his hand shaking with righteous wrath.

And then Stoick's thunderous brow lightened,
he sheathed his sword, and threw back his head in a
tremendous guffaw. He patted his son on the back
affectionately. 'That WOULD be
funny,' he admitted.

---

*'The Thing' was a meeting of all the local
Viking Tribes.

'Very funny,' grinned Big-Boobied Bertha, her great biceps rippling in her amusement. 'Even better than the bathtub-and-underpants idea!'

And the Tribes of Hooligan and Bog-Burglar put away their weapons, their love of a good joke turning away their anger. Tragedy turned to comedy in an instant.

History, you see, is like the interlocking wheels turning in a ticking-thing. Something unexpected happens, some sort of *hiccup*… the wheels are jogged… and then they set off again, beating out the time in a new pattern.

'So there you are then, Madguts!' yelled Stoick the Vast. 'My son has made his demand, and you'll just have to carry it out… No hard feelings, eh?'

Madguts the Murderous shook Stoick's hand, unable to believe his good fortune. He'd thought that he was a dead man for certain.

You couldn't say that he was *happy* at the prospect of standing up in front of 'The Thing' dressed as an ickle pretty shepherdess.

The pride of the Murderous Tribe winced at the thought of it.

But on the whole, it was better than being picked to death by Sky Dragons.

And the Hooligan Tribe made their way down to their ships and returned to Berk.

Going back to Berk now, when they thought they had lost it for ever, in their boats laden with all their belongings, it was as if they were discovering it for the very first time.

A beautiful little island, all lit up under a canopy of stars.

Maybe it was a little rainier on Berk than you might wish for. Perhaps it was a trifle on the windy, boggy, rocky and heathery side. No doubt there were lands with bluer skies and richer soils, somewhere over the horizon. But Berk was the Hooligans' *home*, and perhaps that is what really matters, after all.

EPILOGUE by Hiccup

So that is the story of how I went to the New World.

I crossed thousands and thousands of miles of ocean, starving and baking on the deck of the ship, slew monsters and fought battles with my life hanging on the thinnest of threads... I cheated death so many times on that journey... and then finally, FINALLY, I saw with my very own eyes, the dream land, the imaginary place, that was no dream after all... it WAS true!

Despite what it may look like, the world is not really as flat as a pancake. There is no waterfall at the corners. There are no edges to the globe on which we live and struggle and laugh and die.

The world is a circle that has no end.

I know that, I have been out to the West and seen with my very own eyes the white beaches and lush green trees of America... and yet I never *quite* landed. I was so CLOSE to landing, that if I swam just a *few* hundred metres more, I could have put my foot on American sand.

But I did not.

What Glory it would have been to have discovered America! To have founded an empire there!

265

To have your name live for ever in the history books…
to have little schoolchildren chant your name, saying
*'America was discovered by Hiccup Horrendous Haddock
the Third…'*

But within touching distance of the Ultimate
Quest, I turned back.

I went home. I took the quiet way, back into the
shadows, to be forgotten by future generations.

It may seem to you, perhaps, dear reader, that my
Quest was not a success.

To have travelled so far… such a very long, long,
long way… and at the last minute, within sniffing
distance of the prize… to have *not* discovered America
after all.

What a failure!

But this is not how it seems to me. Again and
again I have been on Quests that I thought were
for one thing, and turned out to be something quite
different.

For it was on that Quest that I first truly
discovered MYSELF, and my destiny.

We were not ready to build a New World.

How can you make a fresh start in a New World
when you are carrying with you on your boat all the
same problems, the same frustrations and inequalities

of the *Old* World?

Let's face it, any country ruled by Norbert called 'The Land of the Nutjobs' would have turned out to have the same problems as the Barbaric Archipelago quicker than you can say the words 'half crazed lunatic carrying a double-headed axe'.

What that trip taught me was just how very many things were wrong with that Old World of ours. And I returned the long, long, way back to the Inner Isles with a new determination. The boy that went into the Atlantic Ocean that day was a very different boy than the one who came out three months, five days and six hours later. I had been immersed in the waters of the Western Seas, and came out a different person.

I had always known that I had, one day, to take over my father's job. I had always felt reluctant, even cross, about this. Always felt that it was something I didn't really want to do. Now, for the first time in my life I really wanted to be a Chief. And not just a Chief, but a KING.

I knew for the first time that *I* was Grimbeard the Ghastly's True Heir... and I would be such an Heir that he had never dreamed of.

I wanted to be a King who would found a New World, not in some misty country far across the seas, but right *here*, right *now*, at home. I would make the Barbaric Archipelago a place in which Might was no longer Right. Where the weaker Tribes could have their say and their vote at 'The Thing'. Where small children would not live in daily fear of death by wolves, by dragons roaming wild, by starvation and by war. Where the rule of Law would apply to bully boys like Snotlout and Nutjob himself. And, the first thing I would do as a King, would be to abolish slavery for ever from the Viking Lands...

The Slavemark has been a great burden to bear, and made my task so much the harder. But Thor was right to give me the Slavemark. I could never rub it away, never forget the promise that I made, because there it was, in indelible purple on the side of my head. Maybe all Kings should bear the Slavemark, to remind them that they should be slaves to their people, rather than the other way around. And to help them never to forget what it feels to be a child... to be small and weak and helpless.

Perhaps my vision does not seem so revolutionary to readers of the Future. But you have to remember the savage wildness of the world in which I grew up. It is quite extraordinary for one small boy with red hair and nothing very remarkable about him to think that he can change the world to that extent.

I did not realise at that time what a gigantic task I was setting myself, what a huge enterprise, so much larger than merely crossing the Western Ocean and back again... How much easier it would have been to have rubbed along as my father had, shrugging at the injustices, closing an eye to the Bad Things... But that way is not my way. My story is all about being a Hero the Hard Way.

We are all not so very different from Norbert the Nutjob. We need a vision of a New World to help us carry on. And in all that I have done, I have been dreaming of those white beaches. All my life I have struggled to found a New World, a better world, for us to live in. I have struggled to make us ready, to make us good enough, to return once again to that country that I saw, long ago, across the sea.

We are still not ready. Maybe we will never be ready. But we are a bit closer now than when I was young.

Now I am an old, old man, the world that I created has no need for dragons. They have retreated from the civilisation that I brought, along with the wolves, and the Berserks, and the monsters of my childhood.

But when I sleep, I am no longer a Great King but a child again. I slip into a longship that sets out across the oceans far far away, sails spread out like dragons' wings.

On and on we sail, unimaginably far. And if the dream is a good one I see again those white beaches, those green trees, with the bluest of blue skies above. Always sailing, sailing, sailing... *never quite reaching...*

Glory comes not to the weak
A treasure land shines out so strong
O Great and Brave and Searching Thor
I *hope* that that was land we saw...
Once before... Long ago...
HO!

This is all stirring stuff, but how is Hiccup going to keep the Slavemark a secret for ever and ever? If Snotlout finds out about it, Hiccup will never get to be a **CHIEF**, *let alone a* **KING**.

And why does Fishlegs appear to have no family?

And is that the last we shall see of that inventive maniac, Norbert the Nutjob? And what about Hiccup's arch-enemy **Alvin the Treacherous**, *who we last saw being swallowed by a Fire-Dragon that dived down into the burning waters of the Earth's core?*

I have a nasty feeling that Alvin might have survived that frightful experience, Thor only knows how...

Watch out for the next volume of Hiccup's memoirs,
How to Break a Dragon's Heart

So many

questions,

and not enough

answers....

This is Cressida, age 9, writing on the island.

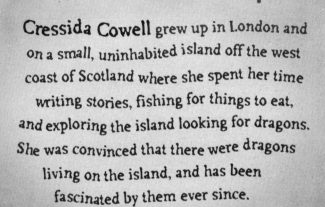

Cressida Cowell grew up in London and on a small, uninhabited island off the west coast of Scotland where she spent her time writing stories, fishing for things to eat, and exploring the island looking for dragons. She was convinced that there were dragons living on the island, and has been fascinated by them ever since.

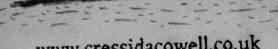

www.cressidacowell.co.uk

HOWDEEDOODEETHERE!

For your latest news on all things dragon
and Cressida Cowell please follow:

 @cressidacowellauthor

 @cressidacowell

 facebook.com/
cressidacowellauthor

Toodleoon for now...

'Exciting adventures, great characters and plenty of jokes and funny drawings make Hiccup's adventures some of our favourite books.' **TBK Magazine**

'Cowell's Dragon books are proper modern classics.' **Sunday Express**

'This series is one of the greatest ever written for those between eight and twelve. Buy them all and your holidays will be blessed with perfect peace.' **The New Statesman**

'Cowell has crafted a modern classic ... every bit as consuming and deep as Harry's in Hogwarts ... And so the fight – part Doctor Who, part biblical epic – begins.' **The BIG Issue**

'One of the greatest pleasures of children's literature. Staggeringly clever and funny mash of Beowulf and Potter, with a truly unusual and "heroic" hero.' **Peter Florence**

'Hilarious and wise, it's never predictable, brilliantly illustrated and always delightful.' **The Times**

'Rollicking fun' **Guardian**

'Cowell's How to Train Your Dragon
books are national treasures.'
Amanda Craig, *The Times*

'Bound to become a modern classic.'
Independent

'Always thrilling, funny and brilliantly
illustrated.' ***Daily Express***

'Cressida Cowell is a splendid story-teller
... young readers are lucky to have her.'
Books for Keeps

'One of the greatest inventions
of modern children's literature.'
Julia Eccleshare, LoverReading4kids

'Funny, outrageous and will lure in the
most reluctant reader.' ***Spectator***

'As with the best children's literature, these books
are about much bigger things: endurance,
loyalty, friendship and love.' ***Daily Telegraph***

'Cowell's loopy scattershot imagination is
as compelling as ever.' ***Financial Times***

CRESSIDA COWELL
HOW TO TRAIN YOUR
DRAGON

**ALSO AVAILABLE IN AUDIO
READ BY THE AWARD-WINNING ACTOR
DAVID TENNANT**

'If you have six to twelve-year-olds, and you don't know
about David Tennant's readings of Cressida Cowell's
How to Train Your Dragon series, you don't deserve to be
a parent ... Simply the best of kids' audio-listening,
and just as much fun for parents.'
The Times

'This kept us all laughing on the edge of our seats.'
Independent on Sunday

AUDIO
Read by
DAVID
TENNANT

Want to listen to an extract?
https://soundcloud.com/hachettekids

h
*Hodder
Children's
Books*

READ HICCUP'S GUIDE TO DRAGON SPECIES ...

Full of dragon profiles and tips on how to ride and train them ... a **MUST READ** for anyone who wants to know more about dragons.